ONE DAY SHE IS LINDA FARLEY, A SENIOR IN A SAN DIEGO high school, with a talent for art, an annoying younger brother, two loving parents, and a prospective boyfriend. Three days later, she is Lainie Foster, hiding with her mother and brother in Olympia, Washington.

That's how fast things change after Linda's mother tells her that her father has been caught by the feds in a Mafia money laundering scheme and that the rest of the family has been placed in the Witness Protection Program. By the rules she's given, she must stay out of school, cut off contact with anyone back home, and never tell anyone what has happened.

Linda—now Lainie—does her best, but in navigating her new life, she faces a number of questions. How could her father do something so contrary to her image of him? Why is her mother so familiar with their new city? How can she pursue a career in art without going to school? What must she do to save her brother from the worst effects of the upheaval? And who is that dark-haired woman she keeps spotting in front of the house?

Then there's the biggest question of all: Is she Linda or is she Lainie? Because, in the end, is the choice really anyone's but hers?

Also by Anne L. Watson

Skeeter: A Cat Tale
Pacific Avenue
Joy
Cassie's Castaways
Willow's Crystal
Benecia's Mirror
A Chambered Nautilus
Departure

ANNE L. WATSON

FLIGHT

Shepard & Piper
Friday Harbor, Washington

For Aaron

Prologue

Some of Olympia's alleys aren't even paved. Just parallel tire tracks drifting through ruts and puddles, crowded by a patchwork line of back fences. I love those alleys, with their overhanging apple branches and tangles of blackberry canes. They're like country roads stitched through the city. I walk ten alley miles for every one on the sidewalk, basking in the sense of peace. I laugh at the acrobatic squirrels and feed my curiosity with glimpses of the candid backs of houses. The alleys are part of my home.

Besides, someone might see me if I walk along the street.

So, I avoid the sidewalks as much as I can. It's easy, since my front door is just off one of those shady alleys. And most of the places where I work are old houses, with gates in their backyards.

Some of my clients don't get it. The second week I worked for Mrs. Clemens, she tried to set me straight.

"You don't have to come to the back door, Lainie," she said. "I never did hold with making the girl come to the back door."

I stifled a laugh. Back in my other life, "girl" was a word Mom taught me not to let people use about me. But what she had in mind—what her whole generation had in mind, as far as I could tell—was men referring that way to women in general. While to Mrs. Clemens, "the girl" was a female servant. It would never have occurred to Mom I could be a "girl" in that sense.

Anyway, I didn't mind. I liked Mrs. Clemens, and I was happy to have the job. Ninety-one was too old to learn to mince words.

"Thanks," I told her. "I wasn't thinking you expected me to come to the back door. But it's a shortcut from my place. And I like to see what needs doing in the yard."

She gave me a shrewd look as I served her breakfast—half a pink grapefruit and two pieces of raisin toast. An old teacher is hard to fool. Back in San Diego, I lied all the time at school, just for the fun of it. Those teachers probably didn't believe me either, but I was too wrapped up in myself to see it. Now everything about me is a lie. My name isn't even Lainie.

It isn't fun anymore. But there's no way to stop.

1
Linda

"Linda, come quick!" Mom called from the yard. I grabbed my book bag and hurried out to see what she wanted.

She stood near a Rose of Sharon bush just outside our kitchen window. In her hand, a baby hummingbird lay crookedly. Its breathing made its iridescent feathers glow gold and green. I looked away. It was so beautiful, I couldn't stand to see any more, in case it died.

"Get the feeder," she said, cupping her hand against its feeble struggles.

I set my bag down in the wet grass and took the hummingbird feeder down from its branch. *No use*, I thought, but I held it over the bird, still trying not to see too much.

"Closer," she said, and I inched it nearer.

She guided the needle-like beak to a feeding hole, and the bird drank greedily. Its eyes flickered to her face fearfully, and it struggled again. This time, it tumbled into the long grass. She bent and scooped it up.

"Again," she said, and I brought the feeder into range. With only a little help, the bird drank more.

"Where did you find it?" I asked.

"Right under the feeder. It must have fallen in the storm."

Not surprising, since the storm had put on a show all night. Rain like a waterfall, and even some lightning, which wasn't that common in San Diego. A tree branch lay in the front yard nearly blocking the drive, and the backyard would be an all-Saturday chore. Our neighborhood was probably *full* of fallen birds that morning, but this was the one we'd found.

"What about its parents?" I asked. Several hummingbirds were hovering around the bush where the feeder usually hung.

"Once they can fly, they don't need them," she said. "If the wing isn't broken, we may be able to save it. Can you find a box? Put something soft in the bottom."

She covered the bird lightly with her free hand as it flailed to escape. I hurried back toward the house, but she called after me.

"Get Andy, would you? He's dressed, and he's had breakfast. I don't know what's keeping him."

I found my younger brother walking around the living room, looking straight down into a mirror he held in front of him.

"What are you doing?" I asked.

"Walking on the ceiling," he said, as if any fool could tell. "Look, the chandelier's a tree!"

He stepped high as he passed through the doorway into the hall, pretending the wall above the door was an obstacle he had to step over. He staggered a bit, but didn't let go of the mirror.

"Give me the mirror, Andy," I said, exasperated. "You're going to fall and get hurt."

"Why?" he asked.

My brother was seven years old, but most of the time I thought he acted like he was about two.

"Because the mirror will break, and you'll cut yourself," I said, grabbing it. He yelled in indignation.

"Come on, Andy," I wheedled. "We have to get to school, and we're going to be late. And Mom found a baby bird. Help me find a box for her to put it in."

"*You* find it," he said. "I don't like birds anymore. They're first cousins to snakes. Mr. Peterson said so." He ran outside.

Mr. Peterson was Andy's teacher, and I had already gathered *he* was first cousin to God, at least in Andy's eyes. If Mr. Peterson had said birds and reptiles were related, it went without saying that Mom and I were going to have to save the baby hummingbird with no help from Andy.

I couldn't find an empty box, so I ripped open a full box of tissues, leaving enough in the bottom for padding while dumping the rest on the cluttered floor of my bedroom. I ran back to the yard and held the ruined box out to Mom.

"Sorry to be so long," I said. "Andy was walking on the ceiling."

Ignoring this bizarre remark, she gently tipped the bird into the box and offered the feeder again. Once again, it drank.

"That's good," she said. "I think it might make it. I'll take it to the zoo after I drop you and Andy off at school. They're sure to know what to do."

"Can't we keep it?" I asked.

"No!" Mom's voice was sharp. "It's illegal to keep a wild bird."

"Even just for a couple of days until it can be on its own? We've done it before."

"Not this time. The zoo will take good care of it."

"But Mom . . ."

"That's enough, Linda. I just don't have time for a baby bird now."

Andy was already in the car, hogging the front seat as usual.

"I'm going to be late," I said.

Mom nodded. "I'll write a note so you won't get in trouble."

Hardly the first time I'd been in trouble at school. But she didn't know about most of the others, so I had to pretend I cared.

I clutched the box with one hand while I retrieved my bag with the other. The bottom of the bag was good and wet, and the books inside probably were, too. Another thing I could care less about—they could dissolve into pulp, as far as I was concerned. I could make a papier-mâché statue out of them. Maybe a little figurine of a good student, so my parents could see what one looked like.

Actually, I wasn't all *that* bad. I aced my art courses—some kind of art was what I wanted to do when I got out of school. I did great in English, too, and even Spanish. But I didn't see any reason to learn math and science now. I figured I'd catch up with them someday if I needed to. And if I didn't, so what?

So it was As in my good subjects and Ds in my bad ones, and I cut a lot of classes. The principal said I had an attitude problem, which was hitting the nail on the head, even if it wasn't particularly helpful. Dad sometimes scolded me about my grades. When Mom gave me a hard time, she more or less stuck to my hairstyle and how I dressed. They specialized.

In the back seat of our Honda, I settled the bird's box on my lap, peeking at it now that I thought it might live. Even without the sun on its feathers, it was shiny in a way I'd never seen before.

In the front seat, Andy hissed loudly and wiggled his arm like a snake. He looked back a few times to see if I was getting it, but I didn't rise to the bait. Mom got in and slammed the door a couple of times before the latch caught.

She started the car and drove around the fallen branch with maybe six inches to spare. Then we headed out into morning traffic.

"Mom," I said.

Her eyes flicked to me in the rearview mirror. "Yes?"

"When is Dad coming home?"

"We'll talk about it tonight," she said.

"But, Mom . . ."

"*Not right now, Linda!*" We drove in silence for a couple of minutes. Finally, she said, in a let's-make-up voice, "How's the bird doing?"

I checked the bird again. It sat calmly in its tissue nest, not keeled over like it was dying.

"He's OK, I think."

Mom glanced my way. "It's a *she*. It's female."

"How can you tell?"

"Plumage," she said.

I figured she knew. She was the one who watched the birds with the binoculars on the kitchen windowsill. Who had an Audubon Society membership and an official Life List. She put out peanuts for squirrels, and raccoons, too, and even took bread down to the beach to feed the gulls and ravens.

Sometimes I wondered if she cared more about wild animals than about us.

"Why can't I be first?" Andy whined. My school was closer to our house than the grade school, so I always got dropped off first. He crabbed about it almost every morning.

This morning, when Mom dropped me off, I waited until she pulled away before I threw her note in the trash. I was a senior that year, and seniors had a few privileges, including occasionally bending the tardiness rules. But I was almost twenty minutes late, and that was pushing it too far. Without a note, I'd probably get a detention. On the other hand, the last thing I needed was for the principal's office to get a close look at her *real* signature after all the times I'd forged it. *Amy Farley*—I'd practiced it over and over, copying her spiral swirl at the beginning of the *A* and her hard downstrokes on both *y*'s. But I had to admit, she did a lot better job of it than I ever could.

My homeroom teacher looked up as I came in. "What was it *this* time, Linda?" he asked. I knew Mr. Fortier liked me, so I didn't mistake his ironic tone for real sarcasm. Just the same, I could have done without his expression, like a little kid settling down for story time.

"My mom and I had to save a baby hummingbird," I said.

He frowned. "What kind of hummingbird was it?" He always asked for details. I was getting pretty good at making them consistent. Unfortunately, this time I was telling the truth. That meant I hadn't really thought my story through.

"I don't know," I said. "Mom said it was a female, on account of its plumage."

"What color was it?" he asked, still testing me.

What color was it? What color *wasn't* it? Chartreuse, with bronze and gold, shining . . . no, *gleaming*. Shimmering. I thought about how I'd looked away from it at first, afraid I'd see the tiny thing collapse into something dull and dead. See it breathe in, breathe out, and then not breathe in again. Tears came to my eyes, and I shook my head.

He wrote out the detention.

2

It got to me that Mr. Fortier thought I was lying *because* I was telling the truth. I was late to homeroom a lot—I didn't necessarily feel like going somewhere just because a bell rang. He'd heard more than a few stories from me, and he usually fell for them. Not this time.

It also bothered me a lot that Mom was so concerned about a hummingbird when she didn't seem to care at all about Dad. He'd been gone for nearly a week, and we hadn't heard from him. Or from her either, on that subject.

I sulked my way through my morning classes, not offering answers even when I knew them. At lunchtime, I took my tray to an empty table and sat at one corner, looking out the window. That wasn't because I was in a bad mood, though. It was what I did every day.

It had started to rain again. I wondered how many birds were lying out there with no one to get in trouble for helping them.

Someone sat across from me, but I didn't look away from the window at first, hoping they'd take the hint and go away. It didn't work. Finally, I gave in and looked to see who it was.

Nicholas. An OK guy, mostly. He lived in my neighborhood. We'd sort of been friends for a few years, off and on. Not close or anything, but in California, a neighbor you even recognize counts as a friend.

"So?" he said. He was in my homeroom, so I knew what he was talking about, but I didn't want to discuss it.

"So, what?" I countered.

"Why was Mr. Fortier on your case?"

"I don't know. I was telling the truth."

He laughed. "Maybe that was the problem."

I didn't know how he'd know something like that, because he got along pretty well in school. He always knew the answers in math class, and he'd had some kind of computer project in the science fair, something about genetics. The only reason he missed being a nerd was that he was the best player on the basketball team.

"Probably," I said. "Mostly, the teachers believe me when I lie."

"Really?"

I thought about it. "Not when I make excuses, like promising to do better in math. But everyone knows that's just conversation."

He laughed again. I was really cracking him up. It pissed me off, so I stood up to go.

"Wait," he said. "I'm sorry. I thought you were joking."

I sat down again, eyeing him warily. "You know what I mean," I said, still half-annoyed. "When the teachers get on one of those things where they have some kind of script or something, you just say your lines. They know it, you know it. Maybe they don't want to be having that conversation any more than you do."

"So what kind of lies do they believe?" he asked.

"The big ones. Like the day I said my dad turned up during lunch and took me out to eat, and I forgot the time. What I was really doing after lunch was hiding in the bathroom."

He looked puzzled. "Why?"

"He was *supposed* to take me out to lunch, but he never showed. I was too upset to go back to class. And then he didn't come home that night, either. Or at all—he's still gone. And Mom won't talk about it."

"Shit," he said. "I'm sorry. I didn't know."

"No one does," I said. "At least, no one's said anything. Including me. I guess I could make an announcement on the PA system. 'Attention, everybody! My dad disappeared!'"

I snorted at my own wit, and coughed back some of the tears I'd been swallowing. Nicholas passed me a glass of water from his tray.

"It's OK," he said. "I didn't drink from it."

Just what I needed. More water. He was trying to be nice, though, so I took a sip and coughed some more.

He shifted the dishes around on his tray, carefully, as if it was some kind of test. "I know this doesn't help," he said, still looking at his tray, "but I almost wish *my* parents would split. At least I wouldn't have to listen to them yelling all the time."

"Mine didn't yell," I said. "Everything was fine. I mean, I *thought* it was. He just didn't come home that night. I asked Mom where he was, and she said, 'I can't discuss that with you right now.' But I guess it's *still* 'right now,' because she won't say any more about it. Longest 'right now' in history. It's weird."

"He never called or anything?"

"No." I looked back outside, feeling tears sting behind my nose. Talking about Dad leaving seemed to make it more real. More like the things that could only happen to other people.

"Hey, you OK?" Nicholas roused me from my little self-pity party.

"Sure," I said. I didn't mean it to sound as sarcastic as it came out.

He gave me a worried look.

"Really," I said. "I mean, I'm upset, but I'm not desperate or anything."

He didn't seem convinced. Maybe I wasn't as good a liar as I thought.

The bell rang for the next classes, and kids thronged to the doors. Nicholas got up.

"Look, I'll meet you after school, OK?" he said. "We can talk some more."

He smiled. I must have seen him smile before, but as he raised one hand in a see-you-later gesture, I really noticed that smile for the first time.

I started to gather my books, and turned to watch him leave the cafeteria, comforted that there was one person I could talk to. But before he reached the door, I'd lost track of him in the crowd.

3

I didn't pay attention in my afternoon classes, and my teachers didn't call on me. They seemed to get that I was in no mood to solve equations or answer questions about the causes of the Vietnam War.

Art was my last class of the day, and I poured everything I felt into a drawing that probably could have been used as evidence to commit me. The art teacher gave me some advice about shading, but didn't mention the subject matter, which was probably just as well.

Nicholas met me at my locker after school, looking pretty relaxed for someone who'd volunteered to get involved in someone else's family hassles.

"Want to walk home?" he asked. "It's not raining anymore."

It was about a mile to our neighborhood, and I usually walked if the weather was halfway decent. "Sure," I said.

I stuffed my homework books into my backpack and draped it over one shoulder. We made our way through the crowded hallways with a few curious looks from people who were probably wondering if we were a couple now. Since I was pretty much a loner, I didn't care what they thought. I tried to look normal, whatever that was—I was starting to forget.

For the first couple of blocks, we walked along without saying anything. San Diego doesn't see much in the way of seasons, not the postcard kind, anyway. Our eucalyptus trees don't turn colors in the fall like trees in New England. The main difference between summer and winter in Southern California is rain. Only the soggy leaves in the gutter reminded me that time was passing, that things changed.

"So, what's going on?" Nicholas finally asked.

"I wish I knew," I said. "Dad just vanished. That's all I can tell you."

"What did your mom tell *you*?"

"Nothing. Well, hardly anything. She said she didn't know when he'd be back."

"So, you don't know *anything*?" He sounded surprised. Since he'd said his parents did a lot of yelling, he at least knew what the problems were.

"No," I said. "I thought maybe he went to Indonesia. He's an engineer, and sometimes he has to go help when there's an earthquake. They've had several lately, and he was talking about going there. But I asked Mom, and she said he didn't."

"Then what do you think *did* happen?"

"I guess he split," I said. I tried to be casual and cool, but my voice broke around a sudden tightness in my throat. "That's the only thing I can think of."

He looked sharply at me. "His car's gone?"

Good question—one I hadn't really thought to consider. "It's not in the driveway, where he usually leaves it. I guess it could be in the garage. I never go in there."

"What about the rest of his stuff? Clothes, computer, stuff like that?"

"I haven't noticed anything missing, but I didn't really look."

"He hasn't phoned or anything?"

"Not that I know of. If Mom talked to him, she didn't say anything about it."

"What about the answering machine?"

"I leave the messages for Mom. Most of them are for her, anyway."

I felt stupid. If I was so upset about what was going on, why hadn't I done more to find out? The answer was, it hadn't even occurred to me. My parents were really good about letting me have my privacy. So spying on them wasn't an option. It wasn't the way my family lived.

I shrugged. "I don't know how I feel about looking through his closet or stuff like that." I didn't want to sound like a goody-goody, but I felt uncomfortable about the whole conversation.

"Yeah, I know," Nicholas said. "But it isn't snooping to check the garage for the car. I guess I wouldn't want to go through my parents' closets or computers, either. It's up to you. Your only other choice is to make your mother tell you what's going on."

"Some choice," I said. We left it at that, and when we got to my house, he just stood and faced me for a breath or two.

"Are you going out with anyone?" he asked.

My throat felt stuck. I cleared it—not a romantic sound.

"No," I said.

"Want to go to a movie or something this weekend?" he asked.

I nodded, and he reached out and gently touched my cheek with one finger.

"I'll call you tonight," he said, and went on up the street toward home. I waited until he was out of sight, then walked up the empty driveway and opened the garage door.

Dad's car was inside.

4

Mom bustled through the kitchen door with Andy on her heels. He dashed past her into the living room and turned on the TV.

"Mom," I said.

"Just a second." She looked into the living room and said, "*One* show, Andrew. Just one, so this had better be the one you want most."

Back in the kitchen, she put a big pot of water on the back burner. Evidently, we were going to have spaghetti again. I took an onion out of the refrigerator and held it up.

"Want this chopped?" I asked. We had spaghetti so often, it was kind of a routine. She nodded, smiling at my helpfulness.

I hated to break the atmosphere, but I had to ask about Dad before the end of Andy's TV show released him back into the world of humans.

"Mom," I said, "Where did Dad go? His car is still in the garage."

She looked quickly toward the living room, but the noise from out there would have blocked the sound of an earthquake.

"I told you I'd explain it to you tonight," she said. "Wait until Andy's in bed."

At least that was progress. I spent the next couple of hours wondering what she was going to say. Dinner dragged by, then Andy's bath, then his story time, his glass of water, all his delaying tactics. I sat in the living room and tried to imagine what Dad could be up to, or what could have happened to him. I toyed with every possibility I could think of, from a nervous breakdown to a mission for the CIA. It all sounded ridiculous.

Finally, Mom came in and sat down.

"I need you to promise not to discuss this with anyone. *Anyone,* OK?"

"OK." I looked down at the nubby tan fabric of the couch rather than into her eyes. When I was little, I'd played on the couch with my toy horses. In my game, the couch was a rocky desert, and the horses jumped from one cushion to the other, afraid they'd get stuck between them.

Mom seemed to be fishing for words, and I was starting to feel a little nervous about where this was heading. I couldn't think of anything to say, so I just waited.

"Your dad . . ." She hesitated. "He got involved with some people in Yuma. It was an immigration thing. People crossing the Mexican border."

"But Dad's an engineer," I said, confused. "What did he do, build a tunnel?"

She smiled, but she didn't look amused at all. "Do you know what money laundering is?"

"Sort of," I said. "It's something criminals do."

"Right," she said. "They need to have a legal source for their money, so they find ways to claim it came from some legitimate business."

"What does that have to do with Dad?" I asked.

"Well, what it comes down to is that your dad was using the company to launder money from an illegal immigration setup. Do you remember on the news a while ago, how a whole truckload of illegal immigrants died?"

I did. The people had been packed into the truck like cattle on their way to market. They'd asphyxiated in the desert heat. The TV news had gone into horrifying detail.

"Yes," I said. "But Dad didn't do that. I mean, he was here."

"Of course he wasn't driving the *truck*," she said. "But . . ." Her voice trailed off.

"But he's partly responsible for what happened," I said slowly.

"Yes," Mom said, watching my face, trying to see how I was taking it. "He was the money man. He was the one who made it possible."

"Where is he?"

"In jail."

I looked down at the couch again. The fabric wasn't anything like a real desert where someone could get trapped without air or water. It was beige upholstery in a middle-class house, that's all.

"I don't know what to say," I told her. "I never would have guessed Dad would do something like that."

"I was pretty upset when I found out, too," Mom said.

"Maybe he didn't do it?" I asked hopefully.

"He confessed."

"Oh." I took that in. Finally, I asked, "Is he going to be in jail for a long time?"

"Of course he is." Mom sounded angry. "You can't do something like that and get away with it."

"Oh." I tried to imagine Dad in jail. I'd never seen a prison, so all I could come up with was a few TV shows. I couldn't put Dad into those scenes at all.

"I'm afraid there's more," Mom said.

I wanted to scream. What else could there possibly be?

"Some of the people he was involved with . . ." She faltered again, but I couldn't finish the sentence for her, this time.

After a long pause, she went on. "They were Las Vegas people, organized crime people. Your dad is going to try to get his sentence reduced by testifying against them. That means we can't stay here now. We have to move somewhere else and change our names. It's part of the Witness Protection Program. You've heard of that?"

I was stunned. "Yes," I said. "But when?"

"As soon as possible," she said. "I can't tell Andy until the last second, because he's too young to remember not to talk about it. So, tomorrow morning, we'll say you're sick, and I'll take him to school. I need your help getting ready."

"But, Mom . . ." I sounded whiny, like a kid Andy's age. But she wasn't listening anyway.

"Your dad has to let them know one way or the other about testifying by the end of the week," she said. "By the time he does, we have to be gone."

"But I have a date this weekend," I said.

"You can't go."

"I have a detention tomorrow."

"You're not going back to school," she said automatically. Then she frowned. "Why did you get a detention?"

"I lost your note about being late. They didn't believe me about the bird."

"Don't worry about it. Linda Farley has a date and a detention. But *you're* Lainie Foster." Then, seeing me sit there with my mouth open, she added, "That's a nickname for Elaine."

In case I needed to know.

5

Lainie

"Why do we have to go to Los Angeles?" I asked. "There's a perfectly good train station and airport in San Diego."

Mom cut across the freeway to the fast lane. "I wish you wouldn't argue so much, Linda," she said. "I mean, Lainie. The stations in L.A. are crowded. No one will notice us there."

"You don't have to start calling me Lainie *yet*, do you?"

"Yes, I do. And you'd better remember to call Andy *Alan*. The marshals will kick us out of Witness Protection if we break the rules."

"Great. Big Brother is watching us."

"Don't forget they're watching *out* for us, too."

"I think I liked freedom better."

Mom gave me an annoyed glance in the rearview mirror. "Unfortunately, *freedom* right now means the freedom to fall into the hands of the Mafia. I don't think you'd like *that* better, Lainie, I really don't."

"Alan" let out a horselaugh. He was having a good time, listening to Mom and me argue. "Lainie, Lainie, pain in the anie," he chortled.

"Stop that, Alan," Mom snapped. "It isn't funny, and I don't want you using that kind of language."

"Why not? Dad said my friend Wally was a 'painus in the anus.' If he can say it, I can say it."

"*No, you can't.* And we are not going to discuss your father anymore, do you understand?"

She glanced back at me again. "I'm taking a chance, letting you travel on your own. But if they're looking for the three of us together, it'll be safer if we split up. But you're not to tell anyone *anything*, do you understand?"

"Mom," I groaned. "I am not Andy . . . *Alan's* . . . age. I get it."

"Don't be calling your friends in San Diego, either. They can trace calls in no time."

"One, I'm not stupid. Two, I don't have any friends."

"What about the boy you had a date with?" she asked suspiciously.

"Well, *that* never got off the ground. And when he finds out about Dad, he won't exactly be interested in me anymore, either. Can't you see him introducing me to his parents? 'Oh, Mom, I want you to meet my girlfriend Linda, the murderer's daughter.'"

"You're not Linda!"

"No," I said bitterly, "I guess I'm not."

She ignored my tone, for once. "Don't contact anyone. And don't be conspicuous in *any* way."

"Check," I said. I'd had more than enough of this conversation.

"Get on the train after almost everyone else has boarded. Sit next to someone who's already taken a seat. That way, you're the one who makes the choice."

"Why couldn't the FBI spring for a sleeper? That way, I wouldn't be next to anyone."

"Too conspicuous," she said.

"Great. I get to inconspicuously sit up all night."

"Stay in crowds," she said. "Don't let anyone corner you for a private conversation. And don't complain."

I didn't ask whether she meant now or after I got on the train.

We sped through a California winter landscape of lush hills stuffed with mini-mansions. By May, at the latest, all the wild grass would be brown, with tended patches standing out like green paint.

"I wish I could have explained to Nicholas," I said. "I really like him, and it was tacky to not even return his call."

"I wish a lot of things, Lainie. Your father took our wishes to prison with him."

She sounded incredibly bitter. I was beginning to realize that my idea that my parents got along was nothing more than that—an idea.

I squirmed in the back seat, trying to get comfortable in my fussy clothes. A total makeover had sounded like fun until Mom made it clear that I had to look completely different from Linda Farley. What that meant was I had to pick new stuff I didn't like—a frilly white dress with tiny red flowers all over it like a case of acne, and a hairdo that made me look like a sorority twit. If this was Lainie Foster, I had a feeling I wasn't going to like her much.

It was better than Mom and my brother, though. She'd teased her hair into a tangle that looked like it came from a cotton candy machine. Her mint green pantsuit and almost-matching bow tie blouse had to be straight from the Salvation Army. The getup was so bad, it made me blink. It was like a trailer-trash grandmother Halloween costume, and Andy—*Alan*—could easily have passed for a child missionary in his new suit and tie. Together, they made a picture that anyone, even a Mafioso, would probably run away from.

"Lainie," Mom said, her voice a little gentler, "we have to follow the rules, whether we like them or not."

"The rules are nuts, Mom," I protested. "Like making us keep our old initials. So the Mafia is too stupid to check the passenger lists for trains and planes leaving Southern California? You think they won't look for two *A.F.*'s and an *L.F.* with one-way tickets to the same place?"

Mom moved to the right to let a tailgating Jeep speed ahead. "That's one reason we're splitting up," she said. "WITSEC has never lost anyone who followed the rules," she said.

"*WITSEC?*" I yelped. "Who the hell is that?"

"The Witness Security Program. That's its other name."

Sheesh. WITSEC. Like the FBI was such a buddy, we needed to give them a nickname. My face itched, and I rubbed it hard.

"Don't do that," Mom said. "You'll rub off your makeup."

"It feels like dirt. I don't know how you put up with it."

"You get used to it. Especially when you have more important things to worry about."

Well, we had that, in spades. I'd just dumped someone I really wanted to go out with. I wouldn't be going to art school next year, because that's what Linda Farley would have done. I had to be someone else, probably forever. Compared to that, grease all over my face really *was* a detail.

I gave up and quit talking about it. Whining wasn't going to do any good. Mom kept quiet too, watching the traffic. In the front seat, Alan sang some dumb song from a TV kids' show, over and over. But, as Mom had said, I had more important things to worry about.

We took the Alameda Street exit and pulled into the train station.

"What are you going to do with the car when you get to the airport?" I asked.

"Leave it in a parking lot with the window down and the keys in the ignition."

Even the Mafia wouldn't have a chance if she did that. The locals would have that car in a chop shop faster than the Godfather could blink.

I got out, staggering a little in my high heels. Mom unloaded my new suitcase, and I waved as she pulled away.

Finally alone in the huge, echoing main hall of Union Station, I thought about calling Nicholas. If I could figure out who might be a federal marshal, I could make a call without being seen. But no one looked likely. I could probably rule out the lady with the screaming twins. Maybe the down-at-the-heels man, checking the ashtrays for smokeable cigarette butts? I gave up. Hell, for all I knew, it could be one of the pigeons flapping around the rafters high overhead.

I snorted. The melodrama was getting to me, but just the same, it was creepy to think of trained watchers out there— the good guys *and* the bad guys. Like some TV show you wouldn't watch any longer than it took to find the channel-change button on the remote.

Bye, Nicholas. I tried to think it hard enough to reach him.

I joined the long line waiting for coach seats on the Coast Starlight. When the train was called, I pulled my suitcase through a long tunnel, jostled by the crowd. I walked slowly, letting a lot of people get ahead, like Mom had told me to. In those shoes, it was easy to fall behind. Every step hurt.

Aboard the train, I wrestled my suitcase into a rack and scanned the car for a safe seatmate. Man or woman? A man might be more likely to be a gangster. Or was it equal opportunity now?

Mafia or not, a man was likely to want to talk to a girl, even a prissy-looking girl like me. At the very least, a guy would probably brag, flirt, and pry. I didn't need that for the next two days. So I chose an elderly lady who looked like she couldn't pass the fitness test for a high-school gym class, let alone qualify for the Mob. Or maybe they didn't have fitness tests? I shook my head sharply. I was starting to get paranoid, and dippy as well.

The old lady smiled a bit tentatively as I sat down.

"Is something the matter, dear?" she asked.

It was such a good question, I was sorry I had to lie.

6

"I'm fine," I told her. "I just got a little confused, getting on the train."

She extended a small, beige-gloved hand for me to shake. "I'm Patricia Samuelson," she said. "I'm pleased to make your acquaintance." Her voice quavered a bit, but her glance was sharp and interested.

"I'm Lainie Foster," I said, taking her hand. "It's nice to meet you."

As the train pulled through the yards, the scratched window showed us piles of rusty junk and then concrete river channels covered with graffiti. A painted question: "Is the glass half full, half empty, or twice as big as it needs to be?" An interesting thought, one that must have used up several spray cans.

A few beautiful bridges slid past, and L.A. was gone. That was what I was leaving behind. I had no idea what was ahead.

A garbled, blurry announcement told us the snack bar car was open. My seatmate stood up.

"I think I'll go get a cup of coffee," she said.

I moved my feet aside so she could sidle past me. Of course, that was the second the train bucked sideways.

"Oh, excuse me!" she said with an embarrassed laugh as she fell into my lap. She tried to stand again, and I caught her a second time.

"Maybe I'd better wait for a station stop," she said.

"I'll be glad to get you a cup of coffee," I said. "Would you like anything to go with it?"

She fumbled in her purse and pulled out a handful of small bills. "Maybe a sandwich? Cheese or tuna if they have it. Do you mind?"

"Not at all," I said, putting her money into the outer pocket of my purse to keep it separate from my own. I made my way to the snack bar and stood in line as the train tested my ability to balance in those heels. I was sure that anyone could guess right away I wasn't used to them. Every bump sent a flash of pain through my feet.

Carrying her coffee and sandwich back to the seat, I nearly fell twice. I got back with the food, though, and gave it to her with her change.

"Thank you, dear," she said.

"You're welcome."

I watched her pull the gloves from her hands, one finger at a time, and carefully fasten them to a clip that dangled from her purse handle on a silver chain.

"Didn't you get anything for yourself?" she asked.

"No, I'm not hungry yet. I'll go a little later."

It was a good thing I'd guessed she might want sugar and cream in her coffee—I'd brought plenty of both, and she used it all. Then she unwrapped the sandwich and set the cellophane carefully to one side.

"I really appreciate your going for me," she said. "I just don't have good balance anymore."

I knew exactly how she felt, but there wasn't any way to say so. "No problem, really," I said.

She took a handkerchief from her purse and laid it in her lap for a napkin—I hadn't thought to bring a paper one.

Starting at one corner of the sandwich, she took one dainty bite after the other, with sips of coffee in between.

I looked away from her picnic, embarrassed for no reason I could put my finger on. On the opposite side of the train, the windows gave a view of the ocean now. I'd rarely bothered to go to the beach when I lived in San Diego, because I could always do it tomorrow. Now I wished I hadn't taken it for granted. I watched the ocean slip by while my seatmate finished her lunch.

"Where are you going, this trip, dear?" she asked, gathering the trash from her meal into a neat pile.

"Up to Washington."

"Oh, that's a long way. I'm getting off in Eugene."

"When do we get there?"

"Around noon tomorrow, if we're on time. My son is meeting me."

"That's nice," I said. I gestured at the trash. "Would you like me to throw that away for you?"

"Oh, *would* you, dear? I'm afraid that it's very difficult for me to walk, with the train jostling and what-not."

"No problem," I said, and took it to the trash chute. Once again, I staggered and nearly lost my balance. A seat next to the luggage rack was empty, and I slid into it for a moment, pulled my suitcase onto my lap, and swapped my heels for a pair of sandals. I wasn't supposed to bring any of my Linda clothes, but Mom had been too busy to watch me pack, and, in my opinion, what she didn't know wouldn't hurt her.

I stood to put my bag away, and the feeling of wearing comfortable shoes was an unbelievable relief. I'd never realized that the moment when something stops hurting could be so blissful.

I went into the restroom, turned back the collar and sleeves of the horrible flowered dress, and washed all the makeup off my face. I had to scrub hard on the mascara—Mom had bought some kind that didn't wash off easily. In the end, I got soap in one eye. It stung, but I didn't care. For the first time all day, I recognized my own face.

Still blinking a bit, I looked in the mirror and straightened the neck of the dress, leaving the two top buttons undone. I rolled my sleeves up a couple of turns, and checked again. It still wasn't an outfit I'd have picked, but at least I didn't look like a total nerd.

I felt a rush of relief. A little bit of Linda was sneaking back.

7

I went back to my seat, careful not to disturb my seatmate, who had settled down for a nap. Another garbled announcement let us know the dining car was serving lunch. A woman and a guy about my age got up from the seats across the aisle and headed in that direction. I decided to go, too. When we got there, the waiter seated the three of us at the same table.

The woman was tall, and she had trouble getting into the tiny booth. I guessed she was about Mom's age, but she seemed much more casual than Mom. She wore jeans and a floppy sweater, and her dark hair was in a long braid down her back. The young guy was kind of sulky. I guessed he was her son. I couldn't think why else she'd put up with him.

She and I exchanged friendly-stranger smiles above our menus. Then I had to rub my eye some more.

"Contacts?" she asked.

"Oh, no," I said. "I washed off my mascara, and I think I got some in my eye."

She raised her eyebrows, still smiling. "Washed it off?"

"My mother brought me to the train this morning. I put some on because she thinks I should wear makeup, but I couldn't stand it anymore."

"I don't blame you," she said, still smiling. She didn't wear makeup herself, so at least she probably understood. "I'm Carol Lopez, by the way. And this is my son, Rafe."

She held out her hand, and I took it for a quick shake. He didn't offer his.

"I'm Lainie Foster." It was beginning to feel more like a role than a lie. Like I was in a movie. I was glad I hadn't blown my line and said Linda Farley. Maybe that was the reason for at least keeping the same first initial—in case you started to say it wrong.

The waiter stopped at our table, and while they ordered, I chose from the menu quickly, so I wouldn't hold things up. When he'd taken my order and left, I saw that Rafe was studying the landscape as if he'd never seen anything like it. But Carol leaned back and gave me a good look.

"Did your mom really make you wear makeup?" she asked. "When I was young, mine never cared much one way or the other. But my grandma lived with us, and she thought makeup meant you were out hooking." She laughed. "I guess I shouldn't be surprised it's the opposite now. Rafe, what do the girls at home do? Do they still wear makeup, or is it more a natural look?"

He shrugged, and said nothing.

Embarrassed at his rudeness, I said quickly, "Oh, well, to my mom, it's a respect thing. You have to dress and groom so other people know you made an effort. I see what she means in a way, but I draw the line at actual pain."

She laughed again. "I would, too," she said. "They used to say you had to suffer to be beautiful. Meaning things like sleeping with your hair in brush rollers and wearing tight shoes. Thank goodness, that's over with."

"I changed to sandals after I got on the train," I said. "My heels were killing me."

She peeked around the table at my feet. "I noticed you in the station, hobbling along. I'm surprised you didn't switch sooner."

"I didn't think of it, I guess."

Probably it wouldn't be a good idea to tell her I was afraid of lurking Mafiosi. It sounded insane. Also, for all I knew, she *was* one, which was even *more* insane. Or maybe the *son* was— maybe the Mafia had a trainee division. If so, he didn't seem cut out for the watching-people part of the job. He could hardly have taken less notice of me if I'd been a gerbil.

"Is your mom meeting you when you get off the train?" Carol asked. "Where are you going, anyway?"

"Olympia, Washington. She's meeting me. I guess I'll have to dress up again before I get off the train. Where are *you* headed?"

"Also Olympia."

"That's a coincidence," I said. My paranoia flared again.

"Not really," she said. "They try to cluster us by destination in the coaches. I think they take off one or two cars somewhere along the way—Sacramento, maybe."

"Oh." So much for paranoia. Maybe.

The waiter came with our sandwiches—chicken for me and veggie burgers for them. I hoped they weren't vegetarian, or at least not the kind who would get offended at me sitting across from them, eating chicken. She didn't look bothered, and he was still pretending I didn't exist.

"Is Olympia your home?" she asked. "Or is this a vacation?"

"Neither, really. I mean, it's going to be my home. We're moving there."

"Interesting. What do your parents do?" she asked.

"My dad's an engineer, and Mom's an interior designer."

"Oh, my husband was an engineer, and I know a few of the firms. Where will your dad be working?"

I stalled, taking a bite out of my sandwich so she wouldn't expect an answer for a second. I put the sandwich down and took a sip of water while she smiled expectantly.

"He has a job with the government," I said. "I don't really know what he'll be doing." *Making license plates, probably.*

"And your mom?"

"She's interviewing for a couple of firms. I don't remember their names." I decided I'd better switch the conversation away from my family. "Do *you* live in Olympia?" I asked.

She nodded. "I grew up in Bremerton, about forty miles to the north, but I moved to Olympia when I got married. I own a senior care agency there now."

She fished in her purse and handed me a card.

"Oh, thanks," I said, taking it automatically and looking it over. "What's a senior care agency?"

"Lining up in-home help so seniors can stay in their homes instead of having to go to rest homes," she said. "It's a lot better, and a lot cheaper, too."

"That sounds really good," I said. "What's Olympia like?"

"Still sort of small-town, but getting bigger fast. We like it there. But we were in Southern California looking at colleges for Rafe. Are you planning to go to college in Olympia?"

"I don't know," I said. "I might take a year or two off and work. I want to go to art school someday."

"Rafe," asked Carol, "do you know of any art schools in Olympia?"

"No idea," he said. He didn't need to add that he couldn't care less.

She turned back to me. "I noticed how good you were with the lady beside you. If you're interested in working with seniors, give me a call. On the other hand, I can't promise you'll make a lot of money for school, because it doesn't pay much."

"Thanks," I said. "I'm not sure what I'm going to do."

I might have been living a total lie, but that one statement was about as rock-solid as truth could get.

I had no idea what I was going to do.

8

It was already dark when the train pulled into Olympia the next evening, four hours late. Mom was even later, so I waited, staring out the windows of the tiny Amtrak station. I couldn't believe this was Olympia. It was supposed to be the state capital, but I didn't see any sign of a city, even a small one. There were a few lights, especially as I looked across the tracks, but in the other direction, it seemed to be open country.

The station was run by volunteers and was only open when a train came in. The embarrassing thing was, one person had to stay with me until Mom got there.

Finally, a car pulled up and Mom jumped out, slamming the door behind her. She bustled through the station doors as if a few seconds would make any difference.

"I'm sorry," she said to the volunteer. "I'm afraid I got lost."

"No problem," he said, but it was obvious he was exhausted and more than ready for me to be taken off his hands.

Mom had shed the frumpy look. Her clothes and hairdo were new, but she looked like herself. I was sorry I'd gone back to my disguise. There wasn't much she could have said if I hadn't.

"Did you have a nice trip?" she asked me.

"It was OK," I said. "Especially when we got into the mountains."

Mom turned back to the volunteer. "Thanks so much for waiting with her."

I felt like a little kid when she spoke for me like that. "Thank you," I mumbled in his direction—also like a little kid. Mom gave me an indulgent smile.

"Well, let's go," she said. "Have you got everything?"

I grabbed my suitcase and started toward the door, limping in the killer shoes. Mom took the handle from me and stepped out stylishly, looking like there was nothing to it. I wobbled behind her, feeling stupid.

Alan waited in the locked car, arms folded.

"Unlock the door," Mom called. She rapped on the window impatiently with one knuckle.

"You said not to," he answered, staring straight ahead. "You said not to open the door for *anyone*."

Evidently his new name didn't go with a new personality any more than mine did. Great.

"Unlock the door this minute, Alan!"

He released the locks, and gave me the evil eye as I got in the back seat. "I had to stay up late and come all the way out here, just because of *you*."

I wasn't impressed. Alan didn't mind staying up late at all. The problem was getting him to bed.

"Do you know where we live?" he asked, twisting halfway around to look me over.

"No," I said. "I don't."

He went back to staring straight ahead. When Mom had my suitcase stowed in the trunk, she got in the car and pulled out of the parking lot onto an empty highway that seemed to lead nowhere.

"Mom," Alan said. "Linda's stupid."

"Stop being a pain in . . ." She stopped abruptly. "Don't say your sister's stupid. It's not nice, and it's not true."

"Linda's so stupid, she doesn't even know where we live," he retorted.

Mom sighed. "Of *course* she doesn't know where we live—she just got here. Also, you're to call her Lainie from now on. Don't forget."

"Lainie, Lainie, pain—"

"That's *enough*, Alan!" Mom snapped.

"My name's not Alan."

"It is now."

"Is not. What if I decide *your* name is Banana Slug? Does that mean it is?"

"You picked the name Alan, remember?"

"I changed my mind."

"We'll discuss it later." Mom's patience seemed about gone.

Alan always knew when he'd pushed her as far as he could get away with. He went back to his stone face impersonation. I stayed out of it, looking out the window to get my first views of Olympia. Soon after we left the station, we at least got to areas that were populated.

Mom glanced at me in the rearview mirror. "What do you think of it?" she asked.

"It looks a lot like Southern California to me," I said.

"Really, it isn't much like California. You won't believe the trees!"

Mom sounded excited, but I couldn't understand why. All I could see was strip malls featuring Pizza Hut, Lowe's, Burger King, Rite Aid—all the usual suspects—mixed with stretches of big new tract houses, all in a row. I didn't comment.

"I'll drive around a little so you can see more," she added.

"I'm kind of tired now, Mom," I said.

"Don't worry. I won't give you the whole tour."

I gave up. It wasn't a big enough deal to get into an argument about. I peered through my window as we came to a long stretch of badly lit highway.

"Don't they have a freeway?" I asked.

"Not around here," Mom said. "It's all highways and local streets."

That was different from California, at least. I knew people in San Diego who would get on the freeway to go a couple of miles—on at one entrance, off at the next exit.

The silence from Alan's corner made me check to see if he was still pouting. I couldn't tell for sure, but he looked asleep, huddled against the car door.

We rounded a curve into what was obviously going to be the city. As we passed through a neighborhood with large houses, Mom waved her hand over to the left.

"Our new place is over there," she said. "We'll come back in a minute, but I wanted you to see the Capitol."

In fact, we were passing it. We went under a narrow bridge and then through a squatty downtown, nearly deserted at that hour. Mom pulled into a parking lot with a good view of the Capitol dome and a sparkle of lights on still water.

"The port and the farmers' market are over in that direction," she said, waving vaguely to her left.

I yawned. "Mom, it's really time for me to crash now. We can go sightseeing tomorrow."

"OK," she said. She started the car and we headed for home, wherever that was.

One thing puzzled me. She'd just arrived in Olympia the day before. So how did she know her way around so well?

9
Rafe

Lainie struck me as a little weird right away. I mean she was nice enough, but the stuff she told us during that lunch in the dining car—it just didn't add up. I never heard of a mother forcing a girl to use makeup. Mostly it was the girls who wanted to, and their mothers had a problem with it.

And what was going on with the shoes? Even if her mother made her wear the stupid heels, why wouldn't she change into her sandals as soon as she was out of sight? Los Angeles Union Station is about the size of a football field, and the floors are marble. How smart could she be, to wear high heels all the way to the train?

Actually, speaking of dumb: How smart could Mom and I be, taking that train to begin with, when we could have flown? Going to L.A. on the Coast Starlight wasn't my idea of a great way to check out colleges. Especially going coach.

Mom must've had a notion that we'd sit in a lounge car, spreading out brochures from different campuses and discussing them over lattes as the coastal scenery sped by. It wasn't like that. The train was noisy and crowded. And grubby.

Mostly I didn't like it because I didn't see any reason for Mom to come at all. It wasn't like I was a freshman—I was transferring out of community college in my junior year. I felt like a fool, having my mother drag me around. By the time we got on the train, I was up to here with the whole thing. I tuned her out and brooded about my father.

There was a lot to brood about. He was dead—that was one thing. Too bad it wasn't the whole problem. No one lives forever. But the way he died was awful.

"Early Alzheimer's," they called it. As if there were some time when you were *supposed* to forget everything you ever knew. Like the only problem with Dad was it happened too soon.

It sneaked up. Dad never had that great a memory to begin with. So I didn't believe Mom when she first told me he sometimes didn't know where he was or what he was doing. Who *could* believe something like that? I thought it was a misunderstanding, and she was making it into a big deal. But then he did it in front of me.

"I don't believe we've met," he said politely one night at dinner in response to some pass-the-butter type of request from Mom.

"You *what?*" she practically shouted. "*Eddie! What* did you say?"

His face was startled, like there'd been an earthquake that only he could feel. It lasted no more than a couple of seconds, and then he tried to pass the whole thing off as a joke.

Ha, ha. But the next time he glazed over like that, Mom dragged him to the doctor. Then there were tests and consultations. Pills, diets, exercises.

He got worse.

I still didn't get it. Not completely. Whenever I saw the blank look, I'd try to bring him back. "I'm Rafe," I'd say.

"Well, of *course* you are," he'd say crossly. "You don't have to tell me *that.*"

But he didn't know me—I could tell. So I stopped reminding him. There was no point. Sometimes "Rafe" was nothing but a word to him, and "son" wouldn't have connected, either. I was anybody—or nobody. Sometimes I wondered if he *wanted* to forget me. Like, maybe he *would* have remembered me if I'd been interested in math and engineering, or good at sports, the way *he* was.

Mom knew a lot about Alzheimer's, and she tried to clue me in. She'd volunteered at the Senior Center in Olympia for years.

"Just because he makes sense at times doesn't mean he really understands," she said. "People with dementia try to cover up, the way you'd fake it if you couldn't remember someone's name."

"How?" I said.

Once in a while, I'd blank out on someone like that. Maybe someone who worked in a store, if I'd see them somewhere else. But those were strangers, really—it didn't matter if I only said hi and let it go at that. I tried to imagine having to do that all day, faking remembering the people closest to me. It gave me chills. It was like some science fiction movie where the aliens suck out most of your brain and you're not *you* anymore.

"You mean they can't remember, but they're smart enough to fool you?" I said.

Mom nodded. "It's the way it works. When I first volunteered at Senior Services, I thought the clients would like to reminisce. I'd ask questions to let them know I was interested in their past. I asked one man how long he'd lived in California, and he said, 'Way too long.' But I tried to go on with the conversation, and I realized I was embarrassing him. He had no idea what *California* meant. He was faking."

"That doesn't make sense," I objected.

"It's exactly what anyone would do in their place."

After a while, I understood. Faking took a different part of the brain from the part you use for everyday life. Once I caught on, I got so I could tell when Dad was doing it—even when I didn't know exactly *how* I knew.

Maybe that's why I had a kind of instinct that Lainie Foster was hiding something. Or it could have been the edgy way she sized people up, the way she checked everyone out like she was expecting trouble.

Of course it wasn't my problem, but I didn't have too much else to think about, sitting on the train. That is, other than Mom's chatter about picking the best college so I could get ahead in life, which was starting to sound like an audio loop. And my own funk, which was pretty much like that, too. Even in a small town like Oly, I'd probably never see this Lainie Foster again, but at least she was something halfway interesting to think about. So, she was what popped into my mind to get Mom off the subject of colleges, the day we went to see Ben.

Ben was a friend of Mom's and Dad's, about their age, but pretty cool. He lived on a sailboat down in the harbor. I'd known him since I was a kid. Mom and I used to crew for him sometimes.

For a while after Dad died, I wondered if they might get together. I wasn't sure how I felt about that. Mom wasn't exactly old, so maybe she *should* marry again.

When I thought about it, though, it wasn't an idea I liked much. It was the only thing I could think of that would make Dad seem really gone, really in the past. Also, even one parent was more than I could take, at the moment. I figured a stepfather would just be interference times two.

Probably Ben didn't even have that kind of idea about Mom. He was a lawyer, and more or less married to his job—

and to that boat of his. He spent every summer cruising on North Star, which sounded like a great life, but I didn't see how another person would fit in.

Either Mom didn't care, or she didn't get it. We kept on hanging out with him, messing around on the boat. We went down to his slip the weekend after the trip to L.A., and right away, she started up about the schools we'd seen, and tried to make the conversation into a roundtable about California colleges.

"Mom picked up a really weird girl on the train," I said. Anything to change the subject, which I was pretty tired of.

"Oh?" said Ben. "What was weird about her?"

"She wasn't weird," Mom said. "Maybe a little eccentric. Just the same, I gave her my card. She was so good with her elderly seatmate, and I think she might be looking for a job."

"Or maybe not," I said, just to mess with her.

"She said she was thinking about it," Mom said, apparently unruffled. "She might work out very well as a caregiver. And . . . Well, I don't know. She sort of intrigued me. Such a nice kid, but something else there, too."

"You'd better make sure she's not a runaway," said Ben. "Or a minor. Honestly, Carol, kids can tie you up in more trouble than you can handle."

"I doubt Lainie Foster will be a problem," she said.

"Not like me," I said nastily.

Mom ignored me. She was getting a lot of practice doing that. But Ben shot me the kind of look I'd seen him turn on fast-moving clouds—a sailor's look, ready for whatever change might be in the wind.

10

Lainie

The morning after we got to Olympia, Andy—no, *Alan*—slammed into my room hours before I would have woken up on my own.

"Out!" I croaked, turning over and covering my head with the pillow.

It didn't work. Most things didn't, with him. He grabbed my pillow and threw it on the floor.

"Mom says you have to get up," he said. "She needs to talk to you."

He pounded around the room in circles until I sat up. I guessed he was pretending to be a herd of some kind of animal—there was too much activity for just one. His step was heavy enough for elephants, but elephants don't clatter, so it was probably horses.

When he saw I was awake, he pranced out, leaving the door open.

I got up, shut the door, and pawed through the mound of clothes I'd thrown onto the bedroom chair when I'd fished my pajamas out of my suitcase the night before. I wasn't sure what Mom expected me to wear. Surely she didn't think I'd put on my fussy new dress to eat breakfast? On the other hand, she didn't know I still had my favorite jeans, so it was probably best not to let her see them yet.

I ducked the issue by slipping into my bathrobe. She had let me keep my old nightclothes, presumably because the Mafia was unlikely to have spies in our house. The only likely suspect would be Alan, and I couldn't imagine the mob tolerating his shenanigans for even a minute.

I'd been too exhausted the night before to pay much attention to the room. Now I looked around quickly, surprised. It didn't look like a rental—it looked lived-in. But it couldn't be a borrowed house, because no one was supposed to know where we were.

The room was comfortably furnished, and the furniture wasn't new, though it was all good—most of it obviously antique. There were curtains at the windows, and Navajo rugs on the hardwood floor. The bookcase was stuffed with books, some of the thin ones lying on their sides on top of the others.

Surely Mom would have mentioned if we were staying with someone. Wouldn't she?

A peek around the curtains showed a tree-lined street. It wasn't raining yet, but rain waited in the dull, cold sky. The houses across the street were big and old, like houses around Balboa Park, back home. It looked like we'd landed in a nice neighborhood.

A swirl of leaves glided by in a gust of wind and rattled along the gutter like trash. I let go of the curtain and turned away with a shiver.

Time to see what was going on and get some idea of what was coming.

Grabbing my toothbrush and comb, I headed down the hall to the bathroom. That looked lived-in, too, same as the bedroom. There were folded towels on the rods, and the shelves were about half full of things like Band-Aids and mouthwash.

The bars of soap, though, were all new, and the only toothbrush besides mine was Alan's Mickey Mouse one. I couldn't decide whether someone else lived here or not.

Still puzzled, I went downstairs and found the kitchen. Mom stood at the stove, scrambling eggs in a frying pan. Alan was sitting at the table, apparently in charge of the toaster.

"Mom," I said, "where did you get this house?"

She looked up from the eggs. "Well, it's not *ours*."

"But, I mean . . . is anyone else living here?"

"No, of course not," she said. "It's for us—part of the program."

"Oh, I see."

I didn't, as a matter of fact. But Mom didn't look like she was about to elaborate. She was concentrating on those eggs pretty hard, considering she'd been cooking for at least thirty years.

At the table, Alan embarked on the fourth or fifth verse of what he called "The Animal Song," an interminable ditty about Noah's ark. Smoke curled lazily from the toaster he was minding. He watched it with detached interest, as if observing an experiment. I decided to do the same.

"Mom," I said, "how did you know your way around Olympia so well? You just got here on Monday."

"Well, I've visited . . ." She broke off and whirled around to see where the smoke was coming from. "*Alan!*" She rushed over to pop up the slices and pull them out. "What do you think you're doing with this *toast*?"

"Burning it," he said happily. "It was bad toast."

"It's certainly bad now!" said Mom, getting back quickly to her eggs, which were now also overdone. "Why in the world did you decide to burn it?"

"I want muffins."

Mom slapped a plate of eggs down in front of Alan. Luckily, the plate was plastic—a china one would have broken.

"We don't have muffins," she said. "Eat your eggs. We have to go enroll you at school."

Alan considered this. He actually liked school. He was a smart kid, which is probably why he was so good at getting into mischief.

"Can I have muffins for dinner?" he asked.

"No. For breakfast tomorrow morning, if you behave yourself today," Mom countered. "Finish your eggs and go get ready."

I helped myself to eggs and ate in silence until he was gone.

"Where's the high school?" I asked. "I guess I have to enroll today, too."

"No, I've decided you'd better not."

I looked at her sharply. Was she about to bring up all my misbehavior at school?

Apparently not. Her expression wasn't accusatory, just determined.

"At Alan's age, children don't notice new classmates much," she said. "They're too self-absorbed. But in high school, it's a different story. You'll cause talk all over town if you turn up mid-year in a senior class."

"You want me to not finish high school?" I was having trouble believing this.

"You don't have to not *finish*. But I've decided you should defer it till next year. We don't know if we're safe yet."

"Don't I *have* to go to school?"

"If you're over sixteen, no. Not if you're working."

"But if I go look for a job, people will notice and comment on that, too."

I didn't know why I was arguing, since I hated school. I hated everything about it—the little cliques, the jocks, even the computer nerds. Nothing interested me but the art and language classes, and they wouldn't graduate you just with those. I didn't care if I never saw the inside of a high school again.

But there was something about Mom's decision I sensed I was going to dislike even more. As she explained, I realized I was right.

"That's true, they would. So the best thing to do, at least for this year, is for you to study and work at home. I'm going to be putting in some long hours, and Alan is far too young to be a latchkey child."

Oh. I was going to drop out of high school and become a—probably unpaid—babysitter. For my demon of a brother.

I decided to cut the best deal I could, since her mind was already made up. "I want to at least take art classes."

"Fine," Mom agreed.

"And no housework," I added. "Not more than my regular chores, I mean. I am *not* the maid."

She looked startled but again just said, "Fine." Then she pushed back her chair, stood, and checked her watch.

"I have to finish getting ready, or we're going to be late." She went into the bathroom and shut the door.

Fine. That's what my mother had told me. Everything was fine, just fine.

Then, why did I feel so not fine at all?

11

Alan came downstairs dressed in bath towels. His getup was halfway between Julius Caesar and Lawrence of Arabia.

"I'm ready," he announced.

I ignored him. He gave up on me and dawdled in the living room, waiting to spring his chosen outfit on Mom. I knew I should tell him to quit horsing around and get dressed, but instead, I went back to my room, determined to miss the whole scene.

I shut the bedroom door behind me and got to work unpacking my suitcase. I unfolded the horrible flowered dress, along with three other new ones that were all too much like the first. I stuck my tongue out at them like a little kid—then arranged them neatly on hangers in the closet. They were awful enough without being wrinkled. Or, God forbid, without me having to iron them.

Underwear, nightclothes, the killer heels. Then my forbidden sandals, sweatshirts, jeans, and T-shirts. A few art supplies—those had been absolutely banned. I hid them on the top shelf of the closet.

The pantyhose I'd started the day in yesterday had a big run down one leg, and I threw them in the wastebasket. Good riddance.

Except for the sweatshirts and jeans, none of my clothes were going to be warm enough—one look out the window had convinced me of that. I'd have to buy a coat soon. Other things too, maybe, like a scarf and boots. Heavy sweaters. I wouldn't be able to go out unless I wrapped up like a mummy. Mafia or no Mafia, I didn't see how I was going to be recognizable anytime before summer. Supposing it was ever summer here.

I heard Alan yelling, but couldn't understand what he said. Mom's voice, sharp and loud, cut him off. Footsteps pounded up the stairs, hesitated by my door, then marched loudly down the wood-floored hall. Drawers slammed, and I thought I heard something being thrown across the room. Shoes dragged back along the hall and down the stairs, till I couldn't hear them any longer.

Then the front door banged, and I heard the car pull out of the driveway. I felt sorry for Alan, and for Mom, too. But if I was going to have to supervise him every day after his school, she'd have to take care of mornings. I couldn't do it all.

When I ventured downstairs, I saw what I'd forgotten. I'd forced Mom to handle Alan, but that's all she'd done. The kitchen looked like it had been bombed. The burnt smell of Alan's toast hung in the air.

I wanted to walk out, but there was nowhere to go. I wanted to go back to my room and read until Mom got home. Let *her* shovel the place out. I wanted to do *anything* except what I did—which was to find an apron and clean up the mess.

The smoky smell was coming from the table, so I started there. First the dishes—I dumped them in the dishpan and left them to soak. Then I cleared out the toaster by upending it, sending a shower of charcoal-colored toast chunks across the table and floor. Probably not the best way to do it, I decided a little too late.

When I'd swept up the mess, I turned to the high-piled sink. I fumed as I scrubbed plates and pans, some of them apparently left over from last night or even before. One pot looked like it had been in the sink for days—maybe since before I'd lost my boyfriend, my home, and my dad.

I pulled my thoughts up short. I was getting into a self-pity party. Maybe I'd better not let that get started—it could only make things worse. No one had planned for things to happen like they had. This was an emergency, and some serious badasses might be after us. I had to help however I could, and right now that meant doing what I was doing: cleaning up the kitchen.

So I made a good job of it. I found a basket of cleaners under the sink and scrubbed the floor and counters. And the stove top, the front of the refrigerator, everything I could reach. I even washed the insides of the windows. And all the time I worked, I felt mad and guilty—just about half and half.

Mad, because it looked like I was going to have to give up almost everything I wanted, and Mom was taking it for granted I would. Guilty because I knew I was one of the *lucky* ones in this whole mess, if I was going to be honest about it. Just the same, I wished I could dump my anger on everyone around me, like Alan did.

"Here comes trouble," Dad would say when Alan started one of his rampages. Yeah, Dad. Here comes trouble. You should know.

If you hadn't done what you did, I'd still be Linda. Alan would still be Andy. And a truckload of people I never met would still have names—Raoul, or Pilar, or Jaime, or even Linda—instead of markers in some cemetery south of the border. Or did they even get those?

The housework finished, I stood at the kitchen window. The storm had moved in while I was working, and gusts of rain streamed across the panes. I rubbed my hands with lotion I'd found in the basket with the cleaners, wondering what I should do next.

A motion caught my eye. It might have been a blowing branch, but for a second, I thought I saw a dark-haired woman standing on the front walk. When I opened the window to get a better look, rain blew in and I shut it quickly.

I looked again, but no one was there. Nothing to see— nothing but prints of my own fingers on the just-cleaned glass.

12

Mom came home a little after noon. She found me in the kitchen, eating lunch and reading a magazine I'd dug out of the living-room bookcase.

I had my back to the window. Even though I was almost sure I'd imagined the woman on the sidewalk, I was seriously creeped out about it. I'd given names to the people in the truck, and then I'd seen someone—or *maybe* seen someone. Except it had to be just a branch.

I really had to get a grip. Things were bad enough without letting my imagination go nuts.

Mom set her purse on the counter but didn't take her jacket off. She looked cold and tired.

"Is there any more tea?" she asked, seeing my steaming cup.

"In the cabinet closest to the stove," I said. "The water in the kettle should still be hot."

She bustled around, making tea, putting a sandwich together. She set them on the table across from me and plopped down in the chair.

"Thanks for cleaning the kitchen," she said. "I had my hands full with Alan, and we were running late."

"No problem," I said warily. I didn't want to get into the subject of whether janitorial work was one of my duties.

She smiled at me and ate a bite of her sandwich. "I'll take you to Alan's school this afternoon," she said. "Then you'll know where it is, and you can go up there and walk him home every day. He gets out at three o'clock."

"I'm going to have to buy a winter coat and some other stuff," I said. "Nothing I have is nearly warm enough."

"I notice you brought your jeans with you," she said, indicating the Linda clothes I'd put on after she left. She didn't mention I'd defied her, but she didn't have to—her tone did it for her.

"I can't wear those dresses here," I said. "I'll freeze. And everyone wears jeans. If the Mafia goes looking for a high-school kid in jeans, they'll have to sort through about a million between San Diego and here."

"OK," she said. "But don't joke about the Mafia, Lainie. We're far from in the clear yet. Your dad really messed things up for us."

"We're not the only ones," I said.

She looked at me sharply, incomprehension in her face.

"The people in the truck," I said. "Compared to them, we got off easy."

"Oh," she said, and sipped her tea. "But you know, Lainie, if they were determined to cross the border, they would have done it some way, and maybe they wouldn't have made it. An awful lot of them don't. We can't give your dad *all* the blame."

"Mom," I said, "I just don't understand it. I thought Dad was . . . well, different."

"I did, too," she said.

"And I thought the two of you got along."

"Lainie," she said, "I think you're old enough to have figured out that marriage isn't like what you see in the movies."

"I know *that*," I said.

"Probably you don't, really." She held up her hand as I started to speak, cutting me off. "I'm sure you know it's not like fairy tales, not *happily ever after*. But my point is, in the movies, or in popular songs, there'd be either a sad ending or a happy one. You'd lose your love or you'd get him. But what if you lost your love *by* getting him?"

"I don't understand," I said.

She sipped her tea again, watching me over the rim of the cup. When she set it down, it clattered in the saucer, as if her hand wasn't steady.

"Time goes on," she said, "and people change a little every day. You don't notice for a while, and by the time you do, the person you loved is gone. Being a mother is the same thing. Your children slip through your fingers like water. The little girl I used to have—she's as gone as if she'd died."

Since she was talking about me, that made me feel even weirder than the woman I'd seen on the walk. Or thought I'd seen.

"What does this have to do with Dad?" I asked.

"Only that I married a boy I met in college, a kind of a sweet, gangly guy. I thought I knew what kind of life I'd have with him, and now he's in federal prison and I'm hiding from the Mafia. It's someone else's life, not mine."

"Isn't that what they mean by 'for better or for worse'?" I asked.

"That wasn't the kind of 'worse' I had in mind," she snapped.

"Are you going to get a divorce?" Oddly, that seemed like a petty detail, when it should have been a big deal.

"I can't," she said. "I'd have to give an address, and there goes our safety."

I pushed my chair back, a sudden rough scrape, and stood behind it, gripping its back with both hands.

"So what happens now?" I blurted, "We just keep hiding? Until when? This is crazy. I can't go to school, you can't get a divorce—when does it end?"

"When your father testifies against the others," Mom said.

"I don't see how," I said. "Even if he goes through with it, how do we know some of them won't still be free? How do we know they won't come looking for us to make us some kind of example? I can see this going on forever."

"You may be right," she said. "I hope not."

That didn't answer my question, but she went upstairs without another word, leaving me to think about the whole bizarre morning—and also to clear up the lunch. The thinking took a lot longer than the cleanup, even if I didn't count my thoughts about bussing dishes one more time, which amounted to an impression that, emergency or no emergency, it could get old fast.

I had more important things to worry about. The main one was that, unless the current situation had upset Mom so much that she wasn't herself, she was weird in ways I'd never imagined.

It wasn't so much that she'd mourn her kids growing up. For all I knew, other women did, too. I might not have heard anyone talk about it, but it wasn't exactly party chatter, either. *"Hi, I'm Angela Foster, and these are my two children. They might as well be dead, since they aren't babies anymore."* No, I could see it was the kind of feeling that parents might have, at least sometimes, and not let on about.

What bugged me was Mom feeling sorrier for herself over that than she did for a whole truckload of people suffocating in the desert. *Those* she dismissed with a rationalization that it probably would have happened anyway. She'd do anything she could to save a baby bird, but *people*—at least *some* people—weren't worth a second thought.

She also seemed to think it was reasonable to ask me to hide out indefinitely. But if she could get a job, and my brother could go to school, what was the big deal about me living a normal life?

The doorbell rang, and I froze like a spider in a flashlight beam.

"Screw this," I said, and I said it good and loud. I hoped Mom *did* hear me.

I strode to the front door, noisy as Alan. And I popped it open without even looking through the peephole.

13

The man who stood on the front porch looked startled for about half a second. Then his face glazed into a Mr. Cool expression—probably his usual look, I thought, sizing him up.

"Lainie?" he said quickly.

I slammed the door in his face and locked it. I had no idea who he was, but he shouldn't be there, knowing my new name and where I lived. My heart made a giant leap and then started to pound. My spit dried up. Everything went slow-mo, unreal as a movie.

I backed down the hall, watching the door as if it might open magically. The phone began to ring, but I didn't dare stop to answer it. When I got to the stairs, I went up quickly and quietly. Thank God that Mom was home.

I knocked and reached for her doorknob. She called "Just a minute!"

I took a deep breath and opened the door a crack. "Mom!" I sort of croaked. "There's a—"

The door pulled open. But instead of letting me in, Mom stalked past me.

"—man outside. At the front door!"

"Honestly, Lainie!" she snapped. She walked downstairs, with me trailing after her.

"Mom! There's a man at the door, and—"

"I *know* there's a man at the door, Lainie!"

I hovered on the stair landing, confused, as she let him in. He glanced up at me, laughing. He folded his cell phone and raised it to me like a champagne glass.

"The world's most original butler!" he said. "Did I scare you?"

I gave him a glare that would have melted glass, stomped upstairs without answering, and slammed my bedroom door good and hard.

In seconds, Mom stomped in without knocking.

"Lainie!" she said. "What is your *problem*?"

I could have given her a fairly long answer to that question, but I just shrugged.

"I want you to come downstairs right now and apologize to Vince."

"What if Vince were to come up here and apologize to *me*?" I said.

She put a hand to her head in a melodramatic, I-can-take-no-more gesture.

"What on earth for?" she said. "*You* have a tantrum and *he's* supposed to apologize?"

"I should have waited around to see if he was one of these Mafia dons you've been telling me to watch out for?" Now that I wasn't scared anymore, I was furious.

"He's obviously nothing of the kind. He's someone from the office. If you don't have any better manners, any better judgment than this, it's no wonder you can't stay out of trouble."

She walked out. A moment later, there was a murmur of conversation downstairs, and I heard his loud laugh. I got up and shut the door.

I checked out the bookcase in the corner and picked up the only book I could see that looked interesting at all—

something about cockatiels. I sat on the bed and read about taming one. Apparently, what you had to do was spend hours and hours shut in the bathroom with the thing, impressing on its bird brain that you were the good guy. Maybe I should get a cockatiel—being holed up with Mom didn't seem to be having that effect on *her*. And it would be nice to have an excuse for staying in solitary.

A little before three o'clock, I heard the front door open and close, then heard voices and a car starting. I figured they were going to get my brother from school. I dressed as warmly as I could and left the house quickly. It was still raining, but not too hard.

I walked along the first street I came to that looked like it was going anywhere—Capitol Avenue. I passed some big churches and the capitol building, but there was nowhere to stop, nothing to do. Cars splashed by, headlights already on in the darkening afternoon. The sidewalks were empty—everyone but me had enough sense to stay indoors.

The rain got worse as I reached a park with a gazebo, so I sheltered there. I sat on the concrete floor of the little building and watched the downpour for a long time. It was like looking through a waterfall.

I wasn't too wet, just my feet and ankles, but the wind pushed through my California clothes and made me shiver. I didn't have my purse, so the Starbucks across the street was no good to me.

"Linda?"

A hoarse whisper from behind me, someone who knew my real name. I jumped up, ready to run if I had to. But it was only my brother. He came up the gazebo steps, looking scared and young. And soaked.

"What are you doing here?" I asked. "Didn't Mom and Vince get you from school?"

"Yeah, but I snuck out the back door about two minutes after we got home," he said.

"Why?"

"He's a pig. And she's a big fat cow." He illustrated his point with a few animal noises.

"Knock it off, Andy," I said. "We have to figure out what to do."

To my surprise, he cut the sound effects.

"How did you find me?" I asked.

"I dunno. I just ran along the street, and I was getting wet, and then I saw this place, so I came over here."

"Is Vince still there?"

He looked doubtful. "I guess so. He was when I left."

"Who is he?" I asked.

"I dunno. Some friend of Mom's."

"Andy, do you know where Mom met him? She's only been here a couple of days. How did she get a friend so quick?"

"I dunno. I don't like him. I want to go home." His voice wobbled, and I knew he was trying not to cry.

"We will as soon as the rain stops."

"I don't mean that house. That's not our house. I mean *home*."

I put my arm around him and we sat down together on the concrete floor, keeping close for warmth. For a change, we were on each other's side.

We watched the rain silently because there was nothing much to say. We both knew that when it let up, we'd have to go back to the house that wasn't ours. It was all we had.

14
Rafe

Before Dad got sick, I hadn't thought too much about my parents. They seemed happy. Everything was pretty normal. If anything, Mom was more easygoing than my friends' mothers.

But as Dad got worse, she had to treat him like a little kid, and then like a baby. And when he was gone, she was sort of in the habit. She turned all that caretaking on me. It drove me nuts.

Plus, it seemed like as soon as he got sick, I started noticing articles about why people get Alzheimer's. All of a sudden, I saw them everywhere, and everyone had a different theory. Maybe it was the way we ate, or something in the water. Maybe it was the pans Mom cooked in. Maybe it was related to mad cow disease. Maybe, maybe, maybe. That kind of article just seems like filler, till it happens to someone in your family.

I got really freaked out trying to figure out why it happened, and I read more and more. Genetics, head injuries, high blood pressure. Maybe even an infection. Maybe it was something I could catch, something other people could catch from me.

That bugged me a lot. So then I didn't want to touch him, or use his dishes, or even be around him much. Mom didn't get it—she just saw me as cold. It wasn't that way at all. I wasn't indifferent. What I was, was helpless.

After she put him in Memory House, the warehouse for Alzheimer's patients, I thought things might settle down.

No more waking up at night to find him gone, calling the cops to be on the lookout for him wandering. At least we could sleep through the night.

But that was still far from the end of it. She meant to spend every waking moment with him, and she expected me to go with her. After the first time, I refused.

"Why?" she asked.

"It's a hellhole," I said.

"It is not! The staff is very good."

"I don't care if everyone there is a cross between Mother Theresa and Florence Nightingale. The place is horrible, and he doesn't even know us, so what's the point?"

"Just because he doesn't connect us with our names doesn't mean he doesn't know us," she said. "He probably doesn't have much longer, and as far as I'm concerned, he needs our love more than ever."

"Well, that's fine for you, but I can't do it," I said. "I don't know him any more than he knows me."

I would sooner have gone straight to hell than go back to Memory House. The place gave me chills. It was full of old people, all of them sick. Almost all of them coughed and drooled, and some even pissed on the floor. You could catch just about anything.

But I knew better than to say anything about germs to Mom. She had to be a big hero, and she expected me to be one, too—either that, or she didn't see the danger. She kept harping on how selfish I was.

That was it: She never quit harping. If it wasn't about Dad, it was "what do you want to be when you grow up?" Like I was ten years old. I knew what I wanted to be—I wanted to be left alone.

As the months passed, and my relationship with Mom went down the toilet, I started hoping Dad would die and get it over with. And then I felt guilty when he did. Like I'd killed him by wishing he was gone. I knew it was a crazy idea, but I couldn't shake it.

All hell broke loose when I refused to go to Dad's funeral.

"Why are you doing this?" she asked in her most dangerous voice.

I shrugged. "I lost my father a long time ago. I didn't even know the man you're burying."

She gave me a frozen look that made me wish I hadn't said that. But it was what I felt, and she did ask. It was like she was giving me two choices: to feel what she wanted me to, or to lie all the time. What if I wasn't willing to do either?

She started her agency a few weeks later. I thought that would give her something to think about besides me, but it didn't help. She had enough energy to run the office, make sure all her old people were getting good care, and run my life, too.

So, by the beginning of my sophomore year in college, she was chafing at the bit to get me into a better one. She was thinking graduate school, even.

"You have to decide on a major," she said. "You can't drift like this."

I knew she had a point, but it was a point I didn't want to hear right then. I was still trying to figure out why Dad had to get sick. So I pushed back.

"What did you have in mind?" I asked. The question was sarcastic, but she took it seriously.

"What about government? All through high school, your history and American government classes were the ones you liked best. "

"Great. I can really see me running for office, or working for one of the crooks who do."

"Don't be so cynical. There are a lot of good people working in government."

"Name two. Name *one*."

"Or what about medicine? You always did well in science."

"Wow. I could be around sick people every day for the rest of my life. Sign me up."

She looked hurt. "You used to want to help people. Where did that go?"

It hadn't gone anywhere. That was exactly what I wanted to do—help people. Be of some use. But I didn't see what that had to do with college. As far as I could see, all college did was train you to be a desk monkey. How did that help anyone?

Go to school, choose a career. Every time I thought about it, I felt like I would get pulled into the kind of life my father had. Go to work, go home. Eat, sleep, go to work again. Saturday, hang out with your son, help him fix his bike. Monday, back to work. Every summer, you get to go on vacation, go to the islands for a week. Then back to work. Go home. Lose your mind. Die.

I could almost see his hands mending my tire that day we worked on my bike in the driveway. I could almost see those island vacations—Dad standing in the wind on the ferry deck, picking his way over a driftwood beach at low tide, watching the breakers on a day when the wind kicked up.

There was one more thing I could almost see, something I only imagined, but as real as a memory: Dad being swept out to sea in an undertow, waving his arms over his head, shouting for help. And me on the shore, frantically trying to find a way to save him. But I couldn't reach him without a boat—and all I had was a bike with a neatly patched rear tire.

15

Lainie

There was no sign of Vince when we got home. Mom came to the kitchen door as we dragged in, giving us a big smile. If she was upset that her seven-year-old had gone walking in the rain alone in a strange neighborhood without telling her, she wasn't showing it. At least, not yet.

"Oh, good, you're home," she said. "I've made soup. Isn't it terrible weather? If it's this cold in November, I just wonder what January will be like."

I had an idea it wouldn't be a lot like January in San Diego, but I kept it to myself. We both went upstairs to our bedrooms, and I put on dry clothes—jeans and a sweatshirt again. If I stuck to the clothes Mom had bought me, I figured I'd be well on my way to pneumonia. My brother headed upstairs, too.

Back in the kitchen, I set the table with brown pottery bowls and plates. Still smiling, Mom filled a matching tureen with a creamy soup made from butternut squash and put it in the center of the table. To go with the soup, she'd made a salad of lettuce and tomatoes, and to top it all off, she drew a pan of corn muffins from the oven.

Green, yellow, red—a traffic light dinner.

"Call Alan, would you?" she asked. Her voice suddenly sounded odd, completely wrong for the "sweet mommy" picture she'd been building.

Uh-oh, I thought. *Here comes the blowup.*

My brother seemed to be expecting trouble, too. He came downstairs slowly and quietly. The usual mischievous gleam was gone from his eyes. I'd often wished he'd give me a break, but now that I had one, I found I didn't want it.

"You got your muffins, buddy," I said, passing him the basket. I was waiting for one of his remarks—maybe "I wanted blueberry, not corn" or "Do I get some tomorrow morning, too?" He took one with no comment at all and set it on the edge of his plate. He didn't even butter it, let alone eat it. Then he picked listlessly at his salad.

"What's the matter?" Mom asked, giving him a sharp look. I guessed this was the prelude to saying we shouldn't have gone out, or blaming me for not getting him from school or something.

"Big day, huh?" I asked him. "What's your new school like?" I tried to send him a thought: *Let's get the subject onto something halfway normal and keep it there.*

"School's OK," he said.

"How's your teacher?" I asked.

"She's OK." Noncommittal, but some of his sparkle came back. I would have bet she was pretty. Or did boys start noticing as young as seven? Most likely, they started at about seven *months.*

"We all need to go shopping," Mom said. "I had no idea it was going to be so *cold.*"

"Do we have to keep dressing like we did on the trip?" I asked carefully.

Mom laughed. "The way you have to bundle up, everyone looks the same on the street here. I don't think we have to worry too much about being recognized now, as long as we don't use our old names or draw attention to ourselves in any way. I thought about what you said, that all the kids wear jeans. Let's just notice what everyone else is doing and fit in."

How I was supposed to fit in when she wouldn't let me go to school, I couldn't imagine. Fit in with who? But at least she seemed to be softening a little about the clothes, so I didn't push it.

A gust of rain slapped the window. Water streamed down the glass like a hose had been turned on it. Mom looked up and shuddered. "I knew it rained a lot here, but I had no idea it was like *this*."

I stared at her for a second, puzzled. She seemed to be far more freaked out about the weather than I could see any reason for.

"We've only just gotten here," I said. "It's just a storm. It'll blow over. Besides, it was raining in San Diego, too."

"Not this kind of rain."

It looked like ordinary rain to me. We had big storms in San Diego, too.

She checked my brother's bowl and plate. He hadn't had more than a couple of mouthfuls. "Is that all you're going to eat?" she asked.

Alan nodded, slid out of his chair, and started for the hallway.

"You should ask to be excused," Mom said.

He looked at her like she'd just crawled out of a spaceship. We'd never asked to be excused from the table.

"It's time the two of you started learning a few manners," she said. "Past time, really."

"Why?" His expression was puzzled.

"So you won't offend people."

I had an idea which "people" she had in mind—Vince the Prince, as I was starting to think of him. We hadn't met anyone else. And if *he* was looking for courteous behavior, he'd better not look in the mirror.

Without answering, my brother slowly backed out of the room. As he pounded up the stairs, Mom turned back to me.

"You're both so insolent," she said. She sounded thoughtful, almost friendly. The difference between her tone and what she said was so bizarre, I wondered if I'd heard her right. I carefully ate a spoonful of the soup, minding my manners.

"Good soup, Mom," I said.

"That's just what I mean," she said.

I tried to see any way that "Good soup, Mom" could be insolent. I hadn't been sarcastic, so I was completely at a loss.

"I'm sorry, I don't understand," I said.

"No, you wouldn't," she shot back. "Since you're playing dumb, let me spell it out for you. I go to all the trouble to plan a good dinner, and neither one of you is here to lend a hand. You're off exploring, or whatever you thought you were doing. And then Alan refuses to eat and doesn't even leave the table politely."

"You've never told him to excuse himself when he leaves the dinner table," I said. "He didn't mean to be rude—he just didn't know."

"That was your dad," she said. "He was the one who thought it was better to be casual. Well, you see where casual got *him*. From now on, I want you two to try some decent manners, not act like a couple of guttersnipes."

"I don't think Alan feels well," I said. "He sounds sort of hoarse. Maybe he's coming down with a cold."

It was like trying to douse a fire with gasoline. She flung her spoon on the table and stood, pushing her chair back with a loud scrape. "I suppose *you're* his mother now," she snapped. "I suppose *you're* the one who knows best."

I stared at her, dumbfounded. Without another word, she turned and left the room. I heard her feet on the stairs, heard her bedroom door slam.

Apparently, cleanup was my job again. I put the dishes in the sink to soak for a few minutes while I tidied the kitchen. An artfully arranged wad of paper towels in the trash can caught my eye. Moving them aside, I found a waxed cardboard carton labeled Pumpkin Soup, a box of "Jiffy" Corn Muffin Mix, and a cellophane bag that had held mixed salad greens.

So much for "all the trouble to plan a good dinner." But if that wasn't what had bugged her, what was? She might feel embarrassed at the way I'd treated Vince, but she'd just met him. He couldn't be important enough for this kind of reaction. So, what was her problem?

When I was done in the kitchen, I turned off the down-stairs lights and locked the front door. Up in my bedroom, I left my door open in case my brother was sick and needed something in the night.

I got into bed, but for a while I just read the cockatiel book. I imagined having a pet like that—it seemed more trouble than it was worth. All the same, I slogged on, learning a lot more about the behavior of cockatiels than I'd ever wanted to know. It was soothing to think about problems I didn't have and couldn't possibly be saddled with.

I heard Mom's door open, and the hallway brightened a little with light filtering from the stairwell. She went downstairs, and I heard her footsteps moving quickly from one room to another. A window opened with a soft screech and quickly closed again.

I was almost asleep when the phone rang just once and then stopped. Maybe the caller had realized it was a wrong number and hung up before anyone could be disturbed. Or else, Mom had picked it up right away and was talking so softly that I couldn't hear, not even a murmur.

Maybe that's why, when I did fall asleep, I dreamed I phoned Nicholas. I told him the whole story, everything we'd done, but he couldn't understand.

"*You're* the one who took Spanish," he whispered. "I didn't. Tell me in English."

The problem was, I *was* speaking English. I tried again, but all I could say was, "*¿Porque estas susurrando?*"—"Why are you whispering?"—but by then, I was, too.

At the other end, I heard him hang up gently, as if he were afraid someone might overhear.

16

When I got up the next morning, the patch of sky in my window was the color of a cornflower, with streamers of cloud like angel hair. Looking out, though, I saw storm clouds moving up from the horizon.

My bedroom door was still open, and I could hear Mom downstairs, singing "The Long and Winding Road." A few years before, we'd done that as a skit on Mother-Daughter Night at Girl Scouts—me in my uniform, complete with backpack and compass, Mom dressed up as a Scout leader. She sang a slightly modified version of the lyrics, and I did a crazy pantomime to go with it, pretending to get lost, get blisters, get rained on, get poison ivy, all the hiking clichés. We'd won the prize for the best act.

I resisted an impulse to dash downstairs and do my part again.

As far as I could see, the long and winding road to Olympia was a one-way street. I couldn't connect with my mother by holding on to who we'd been in San Diego. Something weird was going on with her. I had no idea what to expect from her next. I trusted her singing about as much as I trusted that blue, blue sky.

I dressed quickly and checked on Alan, but his room was empty. Not sick, then—at least *probably* not. Going down to the kitchen, I found him sitting quietly at the table, eating oatmeal with raisins.

I glanced warily at Mom's back as she stood at the stove. He followed my eyes and then shrugged at me. She'd been quiet for a few minutes after rendering the last "Yeah, yeah, yeah" of the song, but now she launched into the "Small World" song from *Gypsy*, hamming it up, imitating Bette Midler. She seemed to be *anyone* that morning—anyone but herself.

On the other hand, that might not be so bad.

"*Small, and funny, and . . . fine,*" she sang. As if on cue, she turned and smiled at me. "How are you this morning, honey?" She had never called me honey before, as far as I remembered.

"OK," I said. *Actually, I'm wondering if you've lost your mind. But I'm OK otherwise.*

"Have some oatmeal," she said, setting one of the brown pottery bowls at my place at the table and sitting down herself. I looked down at a gray mass with raisins dotting it like dead flies.

"Looks good," I said. I sat down and ate. Fish ate dead flies all the time, and it didn't do them any harm. Frogs . . . No, I decided, it's *live* ones that frogs eat. Anyway, whatever they looked like, the things on the oatmeal were raisins. Raisins. I kept my mind on that.

"May I be excused?" Alan said. "I need to get ready for school."

Mom smiled. "Of course," she said. She ruffled his hair as he passed by her chair. I don't think she'd ever done *that* before, either.

When he was gone, she turned to me. "I was thinking. After we take Alan to school, let's have a day at the mall. Warm things for both of us and some work outfits for me."

"Where is it?" I asked.

"School, or the mall?"

"Well, both. I don't know where *anything* is, or hardly anything."

"School is just a few blocks away. The mall is over on the west side of town. But everything's close here."

I'd given up asking and wondering how she knew.

"I think it's going to rain," I said. "How are we going to get there? On the bus?"

"No, we have the car."

The car they'd picked me up at the station in. It was probably part of the program. Like the house. Probably the money that we'd use for today's shopping spree was part of the program, too. I wondered if it would all turn into pumpkins at the stroke of some future midnight.

I wished I was somewhere else, almost *anywhere* else. A day at the mall was the last thing I wanted.

"I don't need a whole lot," I said. "Just a coat, really."

"Can this be my daughter?" she teased.

Actually, I was just wondering something similar: Can this really be my mother?

Looking back, I realized I didn't have many recent memories as fun as that night at the Girl Scouts party. Mom had been weird for a while now. Irritable and unfair one minute, sky-high the next. And really absorbed in herself. I couldn't put a date to when it had happened, but Mom had become like a dropout. A family dropout.

I felt an inside jolt of absolute truth. I must have sat there with a poleaxed expression on my face, because she gave me a sharp look.

"What in the world are you thinking about?" she asked.

"Nothing," I said. She looked unconvinced, so I invented something quickly. "I mean, I think I may be getting a toothache. Or a cavity, anyway. Those raisins are kind of sugary."

"Oh, dear. We'll have to ask about dentists," she said. "Can you take an aspirin for today?"

"Yes," I said. "No problem, really. It was just for a second."

After breakfast, I dawdled over getting dressed, trying to sort things out. My feeling of horror about the people in the truck had gotten stronger since she'd first told me. It was something I couldn't get around. It made me see Dad in a whole different light.

It occurred to me that, for a while before Dad had been arrested, Mom might have known, or at least suspected what he was doing. Maybe tried to stop him or something. With two underage kids, what would she feel she could do if her "wonderful" husband turned criminal? Maybe she felt trapped, afraid of the people he was involved with. For all I knew, she might have been the one who turned him in.

I still couldn't picture Dad being one of the bad guys, but that seemed to be the way it was. Mom had probably kept it all from us as long as she could. It was hardly any wonder she was acting stressed out, now that the whole thing had blown open. What else could have made her change from the mother I'd always had to the way she'd been lately?

The more I thought about it, the more it made sense. I felt dully ashamed, and resolved to quit acting like such a kid.

"Lainie," she called from downstairs. "Are you about ready?"

"Be right there!"

A last check in the mirror, and I was ready. I grabbed my purse and ran downstairs to spend the day with Mom.

17
Rafe

It shouldn't have been a big deal when Mom announced she was going out to dinner with Ben. It *shouldn't* have been. Except that I came unglued.

"What?" I said. "You can't go out on a date. You just can't."

"You *cannot* tell me what to do," she said. "*You* are not *my* parent. It's the other way around, in case you'd forgotten."

"You mean, adults get to do what they want to? Does that mean you'll get off my back about being a doctor?"

"I didn't say you should be a doctor. I just used that as an example."

"That's true," I said. "You did mention other professions. Doctor, lawyer, Indian chief. Hey, I think I'll be an Indian chief!"

"They wouldn't have you. You're not an Indian."

"You mean, I couldn't go to college and study to be an Indian?"

"Of course not. Don't be silly."

"Well, I could no more be a doctor than an Indian. For the same reason. It isn't me."

She sighed. "Suit yourself. You always *could* argue your way through a brick wall. What you've never learned is, winning an argument doesn't make you right."

"Fine. If I remember, the point wasn't even about my career. It was about you starting to date right away. It looks pretty tacky."

"You need to learn one thing about marriage before you get into serious trouble," she said. "A marriage is the business of the couple and nobody else, unless abuse is involved. As it happens—even though it's *not* your business—your dad and I agreed that whichever of us was widowed could remarry with the other's assumed blessing. Not to mention that having dinner with an old friend is a fair distance from remarrying."

"Dad was sick," I said. "He didn't know what he was saying."

"It was something we decided years ago, and restated from time to time over the years. And as far as his illness goes— excuse me, this is the first time I've been sure you even noticed."

"That's not fair."

"Why not?" she said. "You weren't any help to me or any comfort to him. And you're absolutely old enough to have been both."

"I did the best I could."

"If that was your best, I feel sorry for you."

That was the way all our conversations went, more or less. It didn't have to be about her dating. It could be anything. Suddenly, everything was my fault. I was the bad guy every time.

The crazy thing was, I started to believe it myself.

I could understand how that would work if a kid was two years old. If a little kid's mom blamed him for the mess the family was in, he'd probably buy into the idea. But I was twenty, and I was doing it, all the same.

It usually started with how disappointed she was that I hadn't helped more when Dad was sick. It was easy to make me feel guilty about that—so, from her point of view, she had me nailed. What she didn't understand was, I couldn't help it. I really had done my best. I'd stretched to do even better than that. I had no idea why I fell so flat.

It was crazy. I knew better, but everywhere I looked I saw things that might make me sick like Dad. Aluminum pots, saturated fat, head injuries waiting to happen—and germs. I really got sidetracked with the germs.

Then the two ideas ran together—the germs and the guilt. If everything was my fault, maybe Dad had caught Alzheimer's because of something I did. And if I didn't disinfect everything around me, maybe Mom would catch it, too.

While he was still living at home, I made up a bleach solution in a water jug and kept it in my room. It made me feel better to sponge down my bathroom with it, so I started using it there. Then I seemed to need it on everything.

Even after he went to Memory House, I couldn't quit. It didn't make sense—there wasn't even any good evidence that Alzheimer's was an infection. And if there was, I shouldn't have needed to take any precautions after he was gone. I knew it, but I couldn't stop.

It was nuts. Alzheimer's germs didn't exist, except that every surface I saw was suddenly swarming with them.

18

Lainie

Mom came out of the department store dressing room like a model entering a runway.

Approaching a long mirror, she craned her neck to see her back. The dress itself, a slinky silver number, made her look like she'd been dipped in mercury. It didn't have much back—not on top, anyway. The way it was cut, it was obvious you couldn't wear ordinary underwear with it. It did have a long skirt—that was where they'd used the fabric.

"How do I look?" she asked.

Assuming she was expecting an answer from me rather than the mirror, I fished for something she might want to hear.

"Great," I managed. *If that's a work outfit, what in hell kind of work are you doing?* My good resolutions about Mom were sliding fast.

"Will your new job involve a lot of entertaining or conferences or something?" I asked.

"Well, I don't know," she said. "I don't exactly *have* a job yet."

"Oh," I said, sounding stupid. "I thought you were working with Vince. You said he was 'someone from the office.'"

Her face flashed into anger for a second. Then she turned back to the mirror, smoothing the silver skirt.

"Do you think it's too long?" she asked. "I wonder if they do alterations."

"They probably do," I said. "But I really don't think it needs it."

She fiddled with the skirt length again, raising and lowering it about a quarter of an inch at a time.

"Vince works at one of the offices where I applied," she said. "I may or may not take that job."

"I think the skirt is fine," I said.

I shifted my shopping bag to let the handle cut into my other hand for a while. After a couple of hours, I'd acquired some new jeans, turtlenecks, heavy sweaters, and a down jacket. Mom had bought some clothes for office work, but also quite a few more party outfits.

I hoped WITSEC was picking up the bills, since there was no way we could pay for this kind of shopping, considering that Mom didn't even have a job. I wondered how long they were planning to support us, and how many shop-till-you-drop expeditions it would take before they drew the line.

Wasn't it the *mother* who was supposed to worry about stuff like this?

An odd tension in my face made me realize that my expression must be a lot like Mom's when she felt put-upon. Not the way I wanted to look. *Not* who I wanted to be. I worked at the muscles around my mouth, trying to make them feel familiar. I might not have my own house or my own name anymore, but I would be damned if I'd take on someone else's face.

I reminded myself I was supposed to be trying to look at things from Mom's point of view. *Not doing all that well.* I tried to focus on how hard it had to be for her to deal with everything, especially with a couple of kids to take care of.

And maybe I'd been wrong about Dad. Maybe none of this was his fault at all. Maybe he'd come up here soon, or we might even go back to San Diego. Maybe that's what Mom was getting dressed up for.

I didn't know what would happen then. Maybe we could go back to being ourselves. Or, even if we had to be another family, he could get a job in construction or something. No one would ever guess the reason he was so good at his job—that he was really an engineer disguised as a carpenter.

I followed Mom through the mall, thinking of Dad, missing him. I imagined us somewhere different, working it all out somehow. Mom, pretty in her new clothes, Dad somehow making it up to her. I could be a teenager again, back in high school, thinking about dates and parties.

When we got to the mall entrance, Mom stopped short. Setting her bags down, she looked uneasily at rain streaming down the glass. A man with dark blonde hair like Dad's brushed past us without a glance our way, pushed the doors open, popped an umbrella up, and strode away in the downpour.

"We could go get a cup of coffee," I said. "Maybe it'll let up by the time we come back."

"We have to pick up Alan at school," she said.

"That's not until three," I reminded her. "We have a little time."

"OK." She grabbed her shopping bags and turned back to the mall's food court.

"Watch over our bags," she said, setting hers down at an empty table. "I'll get us something to eat."

I sat among our overflowing bags. The mall was surprisingly empty, even for a rainy weekday before the holiday shopping season really got going. It had a damp, used look. A few early, discouraged-looking decorations had been put up—or of course, they might have been left over from last year. They certainly looked it.

Shopping here was obviously not much like shopping in San Diego. I'd never been much of a shopper anyway, so I didn't care, but I suspected Mom might.

She came back with burritos and cokes. As we ate, she regarded me in a detached way.

"I hope Alan isn't going to be too disappointed," she said. "But I'm going to be out of town over Christmas. I hope you can take care of all that."

I hid my surprise.

"Where are you going?" I asked.

"Vince invited me to spend Christmas at the Awahnee."

The grand hotel in Yosemite. Mom had often talked wistfully about spending Christmas there. And Dad had always said it was too expensive, and that you'd have to get reservations nearly a year in advance.

Well, that explained the fancy clothes. Forget about Dad coming back. That obviously wasn't in the program.

"I can handle Christmas for Alan," I said evenly. "Just let me know what I need to do."

Mom smiled. "We can't get too elaborate this year," she said. "So, it shouldn't be that difficult."

I smiled back, thinking fast. If it was true that Christmas reservations at the hotel would have to be made that far in advance, who was Vince originally going with? And also, if Mom was gone on Christmas, she'd miss my birthday too, since it was the next day. She'd evidently forgotten that, and I didn't mention it.

"Well, congratulations," I said, "That's something you've always wanted to do, isn't it?"

"Oh, yes. It'll be so beautiful."

As I ate my burrito, I noticed she was eyeing me critically. "Lift your hair up," she said suddenly, and I did, piling it on top of my head the way I did when I showered.

"Why don't you get it cut?" she said. "It would be different, and it would look really nice."

I ignored the implication that it looked bad like it was. "So many things have changed," I said. "I think I'll leave my hair alone for now."

It came out easy and casual, like I was talking to a friend, someone who could only make suggestions, not tell me what to do. But if I was old enough to quit school, if I was old enough to be responsible for my brother, I figured I was old enough to do my own hair.

Mom let it go. Whether she realized it was important, I couldn't tell.

When we were ready to leave, the weather hadn't improved, but we just made a run for it. By the time we got to the car, the rain was pouring down like it was being thrown at us. We got in as fast as we could, dumping our bags in the back seat. Mom drove back toward the house.

But when we were nearly there, she suddenly sped up and turned the corner.

"I had no idea it was so late," she said. "We'd better get over to Alan's school."

"It's only a little after two," I said. "Isn't everything pretty close?"

"I have to pick up some things at the market first."

Her change of plans would have surprised me more if I hadn't seen the dark-haired woman again when we approached the house.

This time she was sitting on the front porch, waiting.

19

"Who was that?" I asked as we headed toward the market.

"Who was who?" Mom's voice was tight.

"The woman on the porch," I said.

"I didn't see anyone," she said.

I looked at her, but she seemed to be avoiding my eyes. There was hardly any traffic, no cars anywhere near. But she watched the road as carefully as a first-day learner.

"There was a woman sitting on our porch," I persisted. "Didn't you see her? She had dark hair and a black coat."

"There wasn't anyone on our porch," Mom said. "You must have been looking at the wrong house. All the houses on the block are big old bungalows, and they're very similar."

I'd only been in Olympia a few days, but I hadn't left my eyes in San Diego. Our house was about the same size as the ones next door on either side, but it was dark green with a wide white porch. Both the neighboring places had brown shingles on the front. One had a small porch, the other had none at all. I couldn't have made that big a mistake.

But I kept my mouth shut, for once in my life. Challenging Mom was not smart. Not lately. I decided I was on my own to figure out what the hell was going on.

When we got to the market, Mom pushed some money at me and asked me to run in and get milk and eggs—which we didn't need. I dashed through the rain to the front door, splashing twice as much water on myself from stepping in puddles as I avoided by hurrying.

I'd scrapped the optimistic little fantasy I'd worked out while I was getting dressed that morning—Mom as hero, struggling against the consequences of Dad's dark side. And I'd deep-sixed the next one, too—that she was getting all pretty because Dad was coming back. Obviously, she was getting something going with Vince. *And* playing dumb about the woman on the porch. But I had no idea how it all fit together.

I was sure that sending me to get groceries was a dodge to get rid of me for a few minutes, so I decided to get a look at what she was up to. I hurried through the store and grabbed the stuff she'd asked for—and a hot pink umbrella from a display by the check stands. No one was in line to check out, so I didn't even have to wait there. I couldn't have been in the store more than two or three minutes.

I left through a different set of doors than I'd gone in by, and I opened the umbrella to block Mom's view of me as I walked toward the car. It worked. I got close enough to get a good look at her.

When she realized it was me, she did a quick double take and snapped her cell phone shut. So, that was it. She'd wanted to make a call without me hearing.

I opened the passenger door, set the groceries on the floor, and sat down, shaking the umbrella outside so she wouldn't yell at me for getting the seat wet.

"I didn't recognize you!" she said. "Did you buy that umbrella?"

"Uh-huh." I rolled it up carefully, set it on the floor beside the groceries, and shut the door. Fastening my seat belt,

I turned to Mom, waiting for her to start the car. But she just sat staring at me.

"Why did you get it?" she asked.

"The umbrella? I didn't want to get any wetter than I already was."

"But why that color?" she said. "You hate pink."

"That's what they had. Anyway, I like it. It's cheerful looking."

She frowned, so I played dumb.

"The umbrella was on sale," I lied. "It didn't cost much. I'll pay you back when we get home, if you want."

"Don't worry about it," she said. "I didn't realize it was raining so hard—that's the only reason I was surprised."

Since it was raining so hard right in front of her nose, that was a little hard to believe.

"Your change is in the bag," I said. "Is that OK?"

"That's fine." She rearranged her face into a motherly smile and started the car.

When we'd gone a few blocks, she made a left turn as a traffic light turned yellow. "I have to go to the post office," she said.

She drove right to it—no hesitation, no maps, no wrong turns. We parked, and she told me to wait. I offered her the umbrella, and she gave me a funny look, but she took it. By then, water was pounding on the car roof about as hard as in a drive-through car wash.

I guessed the phone call had been about the woman on the porch—probably getting someone to make her leave. If that was what Mom was waiting for, I figured she'd dawdle for a while to be on the safe side. So, I slouched down in the car seat and made myself comfortable.

I played with the car radio for a while, but Olympia didn't seem to have any interesting stations. One had a country singer—a woman who'd been wronged and then managed to get a good band to help tell about it. The next featured a preacher hollering that Jesus had come to save me—but the details were unclear, and I didn't feel like I'd better count on it. I turned the radio off.

There wasn't much to look at, so I kept an eye out for Mafiosi and wondered what Nicholas was doing. Maybe he was touching some other girl's cheek with one finger, just a tiny touch like a butterfly landing on her face. Maybe he was asking her if she was going out with anyone.

Or maybe he was wondering where I was. Maybe he was even trying to find me. I toyed with some romantic fantasies of him coming to Olympia to rescue me from all this weirdness, but they weren't very convincing. Since he didn't even know my name anymore, I figured he wasn't real likely to show up. Even Jesus was a better bet.

Mom came out of the post office in a hurry, slammed the car door as she got in, and backed out jerkily. She drove only a few blocks, then parked in front of a school.

Alan must have been watching for us, because he came running out through the rain. But once he got in the car, he seemed deflated. He said almost nothing on the way home, just looked quietly out the window.

I watched him warily. He didn't look sick to me—he wasn't sniffling or coughing. I wondered if he'd just had a bad day at school. But I was afraid what was bugging him was going home, because it was bugging me, too. And I was ten years older than he was, and much more able to deal with things.

But I had no idea how to help either one of us. I was seriously starting to wonder if Mom was losing her mind—nothing added up, from the Mafia story to Vince. It looked like Dad was gone for good. And on top of all the other craziness, a woman was haunting our house.

Except she wasn't. As we rounded the corner of our street, I saw she had gone. Which was good, as far as it went. But it did sort of leave me wondering where she was now. And why she'd left, and why she'd come in the first place.

Things like that.

20

I went to Carol Lopez's office in early November to see if she'd meant what she said on the train about giving me a job. Too bad the first thing she asked was how old I was.

"Seventeen," I said.

"I can't hire a minor," said Carol. "You're supposed to be in school."

"But I really need a job. And Mom says I can't *go* to school."

"That's not even legal," she said. "Unless you already *have* a job, your parents can't keep you out."

"I do have a *sort-of* job. I'm doing nanny duty for my little brother. I pick him up from school and take care of him. But I have a lot of time before that, and I need to make some money so I can get out of the house—get *both* of us out, if I can. Things at home are sort of weird, to tell you the truth."

This must have all sounded pretty confused, but she seemed to be taking it in. "Then I gather you couldn't get parental permission to work for *me*."

I drew a deep breath. "No."

Carol took a moment to size me up. "When will you be eighteen?"

I smiled. "Next month. The day after Christmas."

"Well, that's not too bad," she said. "It will probably take at least a couple of weeks to do your background check anyway."

Oh, God. Another roadblock. "What's that about?" I asked.

"You have to have a background check to work with seniors. Just to make sure you don't have any outstanding warrants or anything like that."

"Look," I said, "that's not going to work. I guarantee I haven't done anything wrong, but you can't do a background check. I *promise* it wasn't me."

She looked baffled.

"It was my dad . . ." I faltered. "Mom says we have to hide from . . . people who might want to hurt us."

Tears spilled down my face. She passed me a box of Kleenex while she watched me thoughtfully. I figured there was no chance she'd take me now. Maybe I could put up notes on bulletin boards that I'd clean houses or something. I didn't think I could earn enough that way to live on, but *no one* was going to trust me with a regular job if I had no diploma and no ID.

I blew my nose and started gathering my things to go.

"Wait a minute," she said. "I'm trying to think of something."

I perched on the edge of the chair, still clutching my purse.

"I can't hire you through my agency without a background check," she said. "But when you're eighteen, I may be able to help you find something else. Come back at the end of December, if you're still looking for a job."

I blew my nose again. "Are you open on the twenty-sixth?" I asked.

"Yes, I'll be here. But that's your birthday. Won't you be celebrating?"

"No, I won't." *Not this year. I'll be doing housemaid duty plus nanny work, unpaid like always. While Mom has a glamorous day in the snow at Yosemite with her new lover. She's the one who's celebrating, but not my birthday—she's forgotten all about that.*

"I'll see you on the twenty-sixth, then," she said. "What kind of birthday cake would you like?"

21

"Listen, buddy," I said. "We have to talk."

"What'd I do now?" Alan whined.

He slowed his already-dawdling progress along the sidewalk to kick at a pebble. I stopped and waited. At least, for once, it wasn't raining.

"Nothing. I'm not on you for anything," I said. "Really. I'm serious. But we still have to talk."

He squinted suspiciously up at me. I tried to look friendly and trustworthy. Conspiring with a seven-year-old, even a demon like Alan, wasn't going to be easy.

"OK, so what do we need to talk about?" he asked.

"You know my birthday's the day after Christmas, right?"

"So?"

"I'll be eighteen."

"That's old."

"Yeah, ancient." I hesitated. This was where it got difficult. "I'll be old enough to get my own place."

"You're not moving out!" His voice cracked with alarm.

"I'm going to try to," I said. "But if we work it right, maybe you can come, too—at least for most of the time."

"How?" He still sounded scared, and more than a little suspicious. I couldn't blame him. At seven, he had years of living with crazy people ahead of him.

"Mom's got her job," I said. Which was true. She went out to work every morning now, dropping Alan off at school on the way. Of course, she'd done that in San Diego, too.

But there, she got off in time to be home when school let out.

"Yeah," said Alan. "Some job. Working for that dumb guy. *Vince.* I hate him."

Hardly surprising. Vince came over a lot, and he wasn't any nicer to us than in the beginning. Mom didn't stand up for us, either. While he was there, we usually wound up retreating to our rooms.

"Well, it's not like when she was working with Dad. She can't leave the office when you get out of school."

Actually, I didn't know if my brother had noticed, but sometimes Mom didn't get home until morning—just in time to shower and change for the next day of doing whatever she was doing. I wasn't about to discuss that with a seven-year-old.

"So?" He kicked something else—maybe another pebble. Or maybe an imaginary one. Maybe it was just time to kick something.

"She can't leave you on your own, either. So, I'll still pick you up from school. She won't want to hire anyone else."

"Why not?"

"Because I won't charge as much. And anyway, she doesn't know anyone. And I don't think she wants to think about it, either."

"So? If you get me from school, does that mean I get to stay with you?"

"Only until she gets home from work—unless she says you can stay over with me."

He shrugged. "She won't do that."

"I think she will, if we play our cards right. If she knows I *want* you to stay over, she won't let you. So, I'll act like I don't care one way or the other. But there's another thing. If you just hang out in your room like you do now, she won't have any reason to want you somewhere else."

Alan thought that over. "You mean I have to be a brat, so she'll want me to go over to your place?"

He was a lot quicker than I'd given him credit for—I'd thought I'd have to explain it. Maybe I should have known. He'd certainly shown an ability to get around Mom in the past. Just the same, he surprised me.

"Don't be *too* awful," I warned. "You have to stay out of *real* trouble, or she'll just punish you. But it would be good to be underfoot, in a slightly annoying way. Like, she wants to be alone in the living room with Vince the Prince, and you ask to watch some educational TV show. Or every time he comes over to eat, you say you want to help make dinner. Or you go to your room to read a book but keep bouncing out to ask questions about it. More like a nuisance than a brat."

"'Vince the Prince,'" he chortled. "I like that."

"Don't repeat it," I said. "Don't do things to get Mom mad. This is important, Alan. I mean it. If you want to get away from Vince, you have to be careful."

He looked at me anxiously. "What about the Mafia?"

"I don't see where it would make any difference to *them* if I move out. Or whether you're staying at my place or Mom's. I wouldn't worry about them. I doubt they're interested in us. They're probably back in California."

I hoped I was right.

"When are you going?" he asked.

"I'm not sure. I talked to someone who might line up a job for me. I'll have to see what it is and what I can afford for rent."

"Who is it?" He always wanted to know everything. When he grew up, he'd be a lawyer or something like that.

"Someone downtown. Don't tell Mom. I'm going there on my birthday, because this lady can't do anything for me till I'm eighteen. She's making me a cake, too—or anyway, she *said* she was."

That got his attention. "What kind of cake?"

"Chocolate. With chocolate frosting."

"Can I go with you?"

Having him there might not be a bad idea at all. Carol would see I was telling the truth about *him*, anyway. Maybe that would reassure her a little.

"If you keep it a deep dark secret between now and then, you can go," I said.

"Can I practice being a nuisance right away? Or do I have to wait till you leave?"

"Right away is a good idea. That way, I can give you a few pointers. If you need them."

It didn't look like he would, as a matter of fact. Getting what he wanted was second nature to him. I had no idea why I'd thought it might be a problem.

"Should I be a nuisance to you, too?"

"Just about like usual," I said. "Don't overdo it."

22

Since I didn't even know if Carol's job was going to pay enough for me to leave right away, I said nothing to Mom about my plans. I knew she wasn't going to approve. Why would she, when she had an unpaid live-in housekeeper and babysitter?

And she needed me as a babysitter more and more. She rarely came home for dinner, and she started staying out on weekends, too. Her efforts to hide her hot romance with Vince wore thin, and eventually she dropped them. If he was the Prince, she was the Princess. I was the Faithful Retainer, while Alan seemed to have no role at all.

He did a good job of being just enough of a pill to make himself unwelcome without getting into serious trouble. I had a few twinges of guilt about that, because his behavior wasn't doing much for any hope of ever having a decent relationship with Mom. But her own behavior made it clear that hope of that kind was wasted anyway.

Mostly I did maid work, took care of Alan, and dreamed about being on my own. I thought about finding thrift stores so I could get the things I'd need—dishes, a bed, maybe a few pots and pans. Carol might take me to one, or she might know someone who would. I imagined a tiny apartment, maybe downtown over a store, maybe in a rooming house where everyone would be eccentric and fun. I'd paint bright pictures to hang on the walls, and there would be lots of sunshine.

If I was lucky, there were only a few weeks to go. Once I was eighteen, no one could make me go here or there, or live in ways I didn't like. Once I had my own place, I'd be the one who could open or close the door. No one else could say who could visit. Alan could mostly stay with me, and Vince would never be allowed.

And then a funny idea occurred to me. If I could do what I liked, maybe I'd go see Dad. California wasn't *that* far away. I could take a bus or something. If he was in prison, they had to let him see his family, didn't they? Maybe my dreams of it all being a mistake, of him coming back, were stupid, but I still wished I could see him. Even if he did something wrong, he was still my father.

On the other hand, what about the Mafia? Maybe they'd know. Maybe they'd follow me back to Olympia.

Or maybe I could just phone him? That wouldn't cost nearly as much, and it might be safer. But how could I find out where he was? Did they even have to tell me? Who would I ask?

Over the next couple of weeks, I thought a lot about getting in touch with Dad. I couldn't decide one way or the other. Yes, no, maybe so—like a jump-rope rhyme. I couldn't get the idea out of my head, but it scared me, too.

As Thanksgiving approached, I wondered how we were going to celebrate. Mom had always made dinner out of *Gourmet Magazine*, but nowadays she hardly cooked at all. I toyed with the idea of trying to do a traditional feast myself, but I wasn't sure if she'd get angry, like when she accused me of trying to be Alan's mother. I didn't think I could do it anyway. And the idea of a holiday dinner with Vince was almost enough to make me gag.

Mom solved the problem one morning at breakfast.

"I have to be out of town over Thanksgiving," she said, with a little frown. "I don't know what to do about dinner. We've always had such nice ones. Maybe I could take you two out to a restaurant when I get back?"

"You're going somewhere for Thanksgiving?" I asked.

"I have a presentation to give in Dallas the next day. I'm afraid there's no way . . ." She trailed off. "I'm sorry. I know it's hard for you, especially since I'll be gone at Christmas, too. I'll make us an extra-special New Year's dinner to make up for it."

Alan looked indignant, and he stayed sulky until he and Mom left. And in the afternoon, when I met him outside the school, he was fuming.

"I hate that guy," he stormed. "Hate him, hate him, hate him!"

I didn't need to ask who he meant.

"Well, but hang on," I said. "I don't like him, either, but I'd rather not have to sit with him at Thanksgiving dinner!"

"But why can't Mom be with *us* like it was *before*?" His voice cracked with pent-up tears. "Why would *he* have to come?"

"I'm afraid it's both of them or neither, this year," I said. "Tell you what: I'll cook anything you want for Thanksgiving."

"Rocky road ice cream?"

"Anything you like."

"Pizza?"

"If that's what you want."

"I want pepperoni pizza. And rocky road ice cream."

"You got it, buddy," I said. "Now let's think up a special dinner for Vince."

Alan spent the rest of the walk imagining what we would fix for Vince if he came to Thanksgiving dinner. In the end, the menu included worms with mud sauce, Brussels sprouts cooked until they were mushy and gray, and for dessert, frozen old underpants with boogers on top.

He was actually laughing by the time we got home.

23

I had no idea how to make a pizza. There weren't any cookbooks at the house, and of course, Mom had left her collection in San Diego. So, the next day, I went to the library.

I found a couple of cookbooks with pizza recipes and sat down at a table to look them over. My plan was to copy one, since I didn't have a library card. I was trying to figure out which one might be easiest to make, when someone sat across from me.

I looked up. It was the woman from the porch.

Apparently she wasn't expecting this any more than I was, because a look of shock came over her. "Oh, shit," she said in a small, tired voice. "The bitch's daughter."

"Excuse me?" I said, wondering if she was nuts. I felt my heart race, and I had no idea what to do next. I could have run out, but a childish idea stopped me: *I was here first.*

She waved her hand impatiently. "Don't play dumb. You're living there on Columbia Street. With the bitch." Her voice was still low, but her face was turning red. "You're her daughter, right? I've seen you with her lots of times."

That made me feel creepy. I'd only noticed her twice, and I wouldn't have thought she'd been close enough to recognize me later. But she sure enough knew who I was.

"Why do you say Mom is a bitch?" Actually, I wasn't sure I could argue the point, but hearing a stranger say it was still kind of disturbing.

"You really expect me to believe you don't know? Tell me another."

I sighed. "Look, she may or may not be easy to get along with lately, but I don't know of anything she's done to you, *or* why you'd talk this way to a high-school kid."

"High school, my ass," she said. "If you're a high-school kid, why aren't you in school?"

"I'm home-schooled," I said. The last thing I needed was this crazy person getting me busted for truancy just weeks before my eighteenth birthday. "Now, why don't you back up and explain a little more politely just what you're talking about? I haven't done anything to you."

She considered me a moment. "Your mother did," she said, sounding a little more sane. "Your mother stole my husband."

"You mean Vince the Prince?" I said, before I could stop myself.

She snorted. She looked close to tears.

"Sorry," I said. "I can't say I like him much. Anyway, I knew Vince was Mom's boyfriend, but I didn't know he was married."

She showed me the book she'd brought to the table: *How to Do Your Own Divorce in Washington.*

"Where's your father?" she asked.

"I don't know. Something happened. I don't know what it was."

She considered me a little more. "Let's go to a café and talk."

We left our books on the table and walked out to the front parking lot. "I don't have a car right now," she said. I figured the one Mom was driving might be hers, so I didn't comment.

"Is there a café we could walk to?" I asked. "I have to be at my brother's school at three o'clock."

My mind raced as we walked up Capitol Avenue. How much should I tell her? Anything? There was always a chance she was with the Mafia—supposing they really were after us, which I was beginning to wonder about. Setting that aside, she seemed for sure an enemy of Vince, as well as of Mom. I wondered if it was true that the enemy of an enemy counts as a friend.

At a German bakery, she bought us coffee and cheese Danishes, and we sat at a small table in a side room.

"What's your name?" I said abruptly, like a little kid.

"Paula," she said. "Paula Buchanan. But you knew that last part."

"You mean because your last name is the same as Vince's?" I said. "But I don't think I ever *heard* his. I'm telling you, I've had almost nothing to do with him. I don't like him."

"I'm not sure I do, either, anymore," she said.

I didn't know much about divorce and didn't want to increase my knowledge of it, so I didn't answer.

"He doesn't like kids," she said after a moment. "I can see it might be hard for you to live with him."

"He doesn't live with us," I said. "You thought he did?"

"I wasn't sure. I know he has an apartment, but I thought he might have moved in with you. He stopped me from keeping an eye on the place."

First thing I've been grateful to Vince for. She really does sound a little nuts.

"I saw you there a couple of times," I said. "You freaked me out. I thought maybe you were a ghost."

"A ghost? Why would you think that?"

I shrugged. I wasn't about to explain about the truck in the desert.

Looking shamefaced, she fiddled with her coffee cup. "I'm sorry about that. I didn't mean to scare you."

She might be a little crazy, but I didn't think she meant me any harm. "I think Mom and Vince just met," I said. "I don't see how she could have broken up your marriage so fast if it wasn't more or less over."

"Just met!" she said. "Your mother has been making trips up here for a year! You didn't know that?"

I didn't. I felt so stupid. Of course, Mom often traveled, but her trips were supposed to be for business, and I never paid much attention. Anyway, how could I have guessed she was sleeping with some guy in Olympia?

Just the same, I wondered how I'd missed something this obvious. Of *course* she'd been here before we moved—probably a lot. Otherwise, how could she have known her way around? It wasn't something I'd wanted to face, but now that I had to, it only made sense.

Stalling for time to collect myself, I ate a bite of cheese Danish and sipped my coffee. "What did you want to talk to me about?" I asked. "You can't imagine I can tell my mother what to do."

She looked unsure of herself. "Well . . . I wasn't really expecting to talk to you. It's not like I have a speech ready."

I nodded, waiting for her to come out with it. Which she finally did, with a catch in her throat.

"Do you think your mother really intends to stay with my husband? Or is this just some fling to her? I mean, have she and your father split up, or what?"

"They're not getting divorced, if that's what you mean. But I have no idea what she plans to do. She doesn't exactly confide in me."

I decided not to tell Paula about my own plan to get away. I didn't trust her that far. She might not have anything to do with the Mafia, but she was still bad news. On the other hand, I reminded myself, I had almost no resources. She might be someone to stay in touch with.

"Look," I said, "my brother and I are minors, and I probably shouldn't even be talking to you." I knew that would give her some pause—I'd learned that adults were very touchy about that kind of thing. "On the other hand, I might tell you more later, if you give me your phone number."

She recited it, and I wrote it on the back of the bakery receipt. You never know when you might need an ally.

Even a crazy one.

24

On my walk from the bakery to Alan's school, I started thinking seriously about how I was going to clean up the mess Mom had made of my life. I wanted to get out of that house—get my own place and find a job I liked. Maybe go to art school or find a teacher. What I really *didn't* want was to abandon Alan.

Also I wanted to find out what had happened with Dad. And, incidentally, to figure out if the Mafia was really after me.

Deciding I wanted to deal with that last part was one thing, but knowing how to do it was another. Maybe I could phone them and ask? I doubted there would be any listing under the letter M in Olympia's slim phone book. The idea was fun, though. If I could call, would I get a receptionist? What would she say?

"Mafia Services. Good morning!"

"Cosa Nostra Enterprises. We aim to please. And our aim is good!"

Or maybe it would be one of those automated menus. *"Press 1 for murder, 2 for money laundering, 3 for kidnapping children of people who testify against us . . ."*

Better get back to the point, I thought, *and quit joking around.* The point was the Mafia, and funny was a distraction I couldn't afford.

I had no idea if they were really after us. Mom said they were, but I had reason to doubt it. I figured they were pretty efficient, and if they really wanted us, we'd probably already be toast. Or at least we'd have *noticed* something.

Maybe not, though. Legal things got lots of delays, and maybe Dad hadn't even testified yet.

Stalemate.

Then again . . . Maybe I could find out about the legal stuff. Even really notorious arrests and trials were public record, weren't they? Wasn't that why we'd changed our names and moved to a different city—so we could be safe even though the facts about Dad had to be made public?

I hadn't paid much attention to the news back in San Diego, just catching a bit between TV shows. And nothing about it had been on TV here—at least I didn't think so. As for the newspaper, I hadn't read it often there, and not at all here.

But something like testimony about a truckload of dead illegal immigrants must have been all over the news in San Diego. While what had been on my mind here was uncomfortable shoes and whether I had to clean up the kitchen.

How dumb could I be?

I walked by a children's museum on one corner and decided to take Alan there sometime. After crossing the street, the state capitol was on view to my right. I admired the building in a way, but it seemed so removed. Maybe for security? But why couldn't a capitol building be more a part of a town, less set apart? No one was even using the grounds as a park. Maybe in summer they would. I tried to imagine leaves on the trees, people walking dogs or sitting on benches reading the newspaper.

Right, the newspaper. *Focus, Lainie!* Back to the Mafia.

Even if an immigration scandal in Southern California wasn't covered in the Olympia paper, didn't the library have newspapers from all over? Or for that matter, didn't they have computers and an Internet connection?

At the library, I could find out almost *anything* I wanted to know, not just recipes for pizza. I could find out about Dad's trial and his testimony, and I just might get some idea how it was going and how bad the whole thing was. Whether he was even all that important. Then I might have some clue how likely it was that this next clump of bushes hid a gunman from the Mob. It would be nice to not have to guess about things like that.

Tomorrow would definitely include another trip to the library.

25
Rafe

You can run into almost anyone at the Olympia Farmers'
Market, and that's where I next saw Lainie.

It was a raw Saturday in late November, and the market
was bustling toward the holidays. The flowers and summer
vegetables were gone, and the booths were filling up hopefully
with handmade gift stuff—jewelry, clothes, woodcrafts, things
like that. It would go more and more that way until the year's
finale on Christmas Eve. I loved the market and went there
almost every weekend—more to hear the musicians than to
buy anything. Anyway, with Mom on the warpath, I'd go almost
anywhere to get out of the house.

Lainie saw me first. I might not have recognized her—she
looked so different in jeans and a down jacket. A lot better. And
her hair was loose, instead of tweaked into one of those styles
that only girls like, the way she'd had it on the train. Not to
digress, but I never did understand why girls do that—bizarre
fashions and long nails and other stuff most guys think is just
plain gross.

Anyway, she looked pretty good. She had a little boy with
her, too old to be hers. She introduced him as her brother
Alan. I would have just said hi to them and gone on my way,
but her brother had other ideas.

"How old are you?" he asked, fixing me with a critical eye.

Lainie didn't shut him up, which was a point in her favor. Being nice to old ladies *and* her little brother—not everybody I meet has that much class.

"I'm twenty. How old are *you*?" I said.

"Twenty! Wow, that's pretty old! What grade are you in?"

"I'm in college. What grade are *you* in?"

"We're going to get cookies," he said. "Do you want to come with us?"

The kid was a real firecracker. He had a great technique—asked questions but didn't answer them. Considering whether this would work for me when Mom got to ragging on me about colleges, I went to the bakery booth with them and joined them at a table.

"You didn't get anything," Lainie said as we sat down. "Would you like half my cookie?"

I looked at it and saw germs. People had handled it, and I hadn't been watching to see if they used gloves. And anyway, who said gloves were clean? And it wasn't just gloves. What if someone had sneezed? If someone in the booth had a cold, they'd make half the town sick. And what if they had something worse?

"No, thanks," I said. "I'm not hungry."

Alan shrugged. "Too bad." He took a bite of his cookie. "They're good."

I could believe it. They smelled great. I wished I could be more like these two, more like I was before. No point talking about it.

"Where do you live?" I asked them.

Alan looked at his sister like he wasn't sure.

"Over by the capitol," she said.

"Did your mom get a job?"

"Oh, yes. She's working for an interior design firm."

"And your dad works for the state?"

"Yes. This is a great farmers' market. Is it open all year?"

The little boy wasn't the only one who dodged questions. She'd changed the subject lightning fast, and there were plenty of signs posted that answered her question about the market. She could hardly have missed them.

"No," I said. "The last day is Christmas Eve. It reopens some time in the spring." Once again, I found myself wondering about her, but I decided it was none of my business.

"Hey, your mom really might help me get a job," she said. "She told me to come back at the end of December, when I'm eighteen."

Well, that was interesting. Mom must be going through one of her stretches where she was desperate for caregivers.

"You know," I said, "working with old people isn't going to be easy."

"I didn't expect an *easy* job," she said—a little testily, I thought.

"OK, OK, no offense," I said. "But old people . . . You might have to do some pretty unpleasant stuff."

"You mean change diapers, right? Well, someone changed *your* diapers for a year or two, or you'd never have made it to potty training age. Women have been changing kids' diapers for centuries. What difference does it make if the other person is big or little?"

I got enough lectures at home. I didn't need another one from a weird girl Mom had picked up on a train.

"None, I guess. Nice talking to you," I said, and got out of there.

26

Lainie

I went to Carol's office on December 26th. I had no choice but to take Alan, so I made him promise to be good. That wasn't too hard, with the prospect of chocolate cake.

I hoped a surprise guest wouldn't be a problem, but Carol had invited one herself. An old lady, skinny and a little stooped, with sharp, bright eyes like a sparrow.

"This is my friend Matilda Hollister," Carol said.

"Mattie to my friends," said the old lady, extending her hand.

I shook her hand and introduced Alan and myself.

"She's here to help us decide how you can work things out," said Carol. "But first, the celebration!"

She unpacked a chocolate cake from a bakery box and arranged eighteen candles on it. She and Mattie sang "Happy Birthday" rather hoarsely, and Alan chimed in with a clear soprano.

I blew out the candles.

"Now you're a real grown-up," Carol said. "What's next?"

"Eating cake!" Alan said.

We all laughed, and I cut slices and handed them around on paper party plates.

When everyone was served, Mattie spoke up. "Carol told me about you a couple of weeks ago, and I've been thinking. Maybe we can put together something that would be good for both of us."

"What do you have in mind?" I asked.

"I need a helper," Mattie said. "Mostly cleaning, a little cooking. And I have a cottage in my backyard—sort of a studio apartment. I could fix it up for you to stay in. Well, several of us could fix it up together. I'd set up a work party."

"Did Carol tell you I have to meet Alan after school?" I asked.

"Yes," said Mattie. "I think this will work. I live right in town, so it shouldn't be a problem for you."

I felt as if I'd been given a million dollars, and I must have looked it.

Mattie put up a hand. "There's more to this deal, though. Carol says you haven't finished high school. And doing that is important. Tell me, what is it you want to do with your life?"

"I'd like to go to art school," I said. "At least, that's what I wanted before things sort of fell apart at home."

Mattie nodded. "All right, then, here's my offer. I have the cottage and what's really a part-time job. We can arrange a barter—your help in exchange for rent, more or less. Of course, you'll need more than that. But I know a few other older people who could use help. Most are retired teachers like me. What I'm proposing is that you work for them, too. We've already discussed it, and they're willing to give you a try."

"That's wonderful!" I said.

She went on. "Again, it would be mostly housework, gardening, general work—whatever they need. They can't pay a lot, but enough for you to get by. But we have one condition. You'd have to work toward your high school diploma by studying for the GED. Like I said, we're mostly teachers, so we can coach you for the test. And maybe we can even find someone to help you with art, now we know that's your interest.

"Anyway, you do need to graduate high school. Otherwise, you'll never be able to get any kind of real job. Or get into a decent art school. Are you any good, by the way?"

A heck of a direct way to put it. I really liked her, I decided.

"Well . . . I think I could be. I mean, it's hard to say, but I think so."

Mattie cleared her throat, looking a bit embarrassed. "I suppose we'll see. The cottage has good light, so you'll be able to paint and draw there. It's not bad, really, but it does need some repairs. Like I said, I can get a few people to help, and I'll buy paint and whatnot."

It sounded great. At least I'd get away from Mom and Vince. Even if I had to work my butt off, I was willing to do it.

Alan interrupted my thoughts. "May I have another piece of cake, please?"

Carol stood up, closing the cake box firmly. "Not before dinner. But since it's Lainie's cake, she can take it home, and I bet she'll be willing to share."

27

"You're *what*?"

Mom sat across from me at the kitchen table, spoonful of soup halfway to her mouth—which was open about wide enough to have fitted the whole bowl.

Alan looked from one of us to the other, like he was watching a tennis match.

"I have a cottage," I said again. "I'm moving next week."

She set the spoon back in the bowl. After a moment, her mouth closed, too. So much for eating her soup.

"You can't just move out!"

She sounded like she was on the verge of another of her rages, and I braced myself. Let her rage. She'd see it differently when she calmed down.

"Actually, I can," I said calmly. I'd more or less rehearsed my part in this discussion, since I'd expected it to be fairly predictable. "My eighteenth birthday was the day after Christmas. You were out of town, so you missed the party."

"You can't afford a place of your own!"

"Actually," I repeated, "I can. I have a job."

"Doing what?"

"Senior care," I said. It was a term I'd learned from Carol.

"What? Where?"

"In home." Another Carol term. "I'll be working for different people around town."

"But you have to meet Alan after school!"

She looked at Alan to see if she could bring him in as an ally. But I'd warned him to stay out of it, and he retreated to studying his soup, avoiding Mom's eyes.

"I'll still do daycare for him, if you want me to," I said. "I don't know the going rate for that, but since he's my brother, I'll give you a good discount."

The mouth opened again. And shut. And frowned.

"You'll be changing old people's diapers," she said. "I don't imagine you'll like that."

"We'll see." Why was everyone so hung up on diapers? You almost couldn't mention old people without hearing about them. I'd changed Alan more than once when he was a baby, and it wasn't fun, but it was just something I'd done and forgotten about.

Anyway, I sure enough wanted to get away from Mom and Vince enough to change diapers, if that was the way to do it. And what job *didn't* have stuff you'd rather not do?

"And that's *all* you'll do for the rest of your life, if you don't finish high school."

Which was rich, considering she was the one who'd pulled me out.

"The people I'm working for are retired teachers," I said. "They'll be coaching me for the GED."

Desperate, she pulled out her trump card, the one I'd been expecting. "The Mafia will find you in no time."

I still had no idea what to think about her claim that the Mob was after us. My research about Dad's trial had turned into a dead end. I'd found the original news story from when the truck had been discovered, a few follow-up items, and then nothing. I'd been to the library several times, working on different ideas that occurred to me, but nothing had panned out.

But I still had an answer for her. "Why would they be more likely to find me there than here? And if they do come after us here, what protection would we be for each other? You're out of town a lot, and neither of us packs a gun. So, what difference could it make?"

I waited for Mom to collect her thoughts. She didn't have much time. She was going out with Vince after dinner, and I suspected she'd be out all night.

"I'll think about it," she said. Her tone was the same as it had always been when I'd asked for permission. She didn't realize—yet—that I'd never need permission from her again.

"I'm sure you will," I said evenly.

We finished dinner with little more to say. Mom sulked and acted put-upon, like I used to back in San Diego when I didn't get my way. She put her dishes in the sink with a hard click—not quite a slam—and started upstairs to get ready. Even though she wore soft shoes, each step on the stairs made a sound as sharp as a slamming door. And when she came back down in her silver dress and four-inch heels to match, each step was like a shot.

If the Mafia guy had chosen that moment to open fire on us, I doubt I would have noticed.

Mom said nothing at all to me as she passed the kitchen— where I was still cleaning up—on her way to the front door. But I was betting she'd feel completely different after discussing things with Vince. He, at least, would be pleased to get rid of me. And of Alan, too, as much as possible. When Mom came back from her date, she'd be full of enthusiasm, maybe even helpful. Another day, another act—this time, putting a good face on Vince's wish that she didn't have kids.

I could afford to wait her out.

When Mom was gone, Alan went upstairs for his bath. Usually, he stayed in his bedroom after that, but this night, he came back down again in his pajamas.

"Is she really going to let me stay with you?" he asked.

"I'm pretty sure she will," I said.

"But what if she doesn't?"

"Won't happen, buddy," I said. "Don't worry about it."

He still looked worried. He was so different from the goofy, carefree kid of a few months ago. Of course, he wasn't the only one who had changed. Mom acted like she'd been invaded by aliens, like in one of those tacky movies where you're just a shell of yourself, with some laser-eyed space creature inside.

I brushed that thought aside—partly because it was childish, and partly because, childish or not, it was close enough to what was really happening to give me goose bumps. If that was what happened to women who fell in love, I'd rather be an old maid. Nothing—no one—could be worth turning into someone else.

I wondered how much *I'd* changed in the past few months. I didn't feel different—not inside. On the other hand, it was probably another story from Mom's point of view. I sighed. Maybe I *was* different—more grown up, but not in a good way. Tougher, maybe. I wondered if it was permanent. I doubted I could ever be Linda again, but maybe I could be more like her, once I got away from Mom.

Alan leaned against me. "Everything's so awful." I could tell by his voice he was near tears.

"It is now," I said. "It wasn't before, was it?"

"No," he said. "Can we be like before?"

"I don't think so," I said. "But if it was OK before, and it's not good now, it changed, didn't it?"

"Yeah," he said. "Some change."

"But, see what I mean? Things change. It happens all the time. They're going to change again, OK? Not back the way they were, but better than now."

It was all I had to offer him—or myself.

28

It was raining the next weekend on the day of the work party, but around here, that didn't seem to slow anything down. In fact, work seemed already well along when Carol, Alan, and I arrived at the cottage—just one big room, really, with a kitchen squeezed into one corner and a bathroom visible through an open door in another. Though no one but Mattie was there yet, the inside was all ready for painting. Newspapers covered the floor, and there were enough humps under tarps to assure me the place had a little furniture.

"We got started yesterday afternoon," Mattie explained. She didn't mention who she meant by "we," but she had said there'd be helpers, so I didn't pay much attention. I was too eager to check out my new home.

The place had lots of windows, even if they only had a view of the unpaved alley and the backyard across from it. It would feel nice when it was fixed up—but those window frames were going to need a lot of painting to make them look good. I figured I'd better start with that, once I'd gotten Alan settled with the bag of books and toys I'd brought to keep him occupied.

Mattie had another plan. "Alan," she said seriously. "We really need your help."

He looked a little suspicious, but she went on without a break.

"I really need someone to put tape on the walls and floor."

He looked at her like she must be joking. "Put tape on the walls? And the *floor*?"

"Right," she said. "We have to do it so the paint won't go where we don't want it."

She tore a length of masking tape off a roll and showed him how to press it on the wall just above the baseboard.

He made a halfhearted try to copy her.

"Great!" she said. "I wasn't positive you were old enough to handle this, but now I see you'll do fine."

Suddenly his interest increased, and he got to work. Mattie winked at me.

"We have snacks for later," she told him.

He looked up from taping. "What kind of snacks?"

"Mmm . . . it's a surprise," she said. "But I wanted to let all the workers see how much I appreciate what they're doing, so they're pretty good snacks."

Alan went back to work, completely won over.

There was the sound of a vehicle pulling up and parking in the alley, and then the sound of doors opening and closing. When I looked out, Rafe and a guy about Carol's age were coming up to the cottage, carrying a ladder.

Mattie introduced the older man as Ben. I wasn't sure if he was Carol's boyfriend or not, but I sort of got that impression. I wasn't that thrilled about seeing Rafe again—he'd been really snotty every time I'd talked to him. I decided to be polite, but to stay away from him if I could.

"Why don't you help Alan with that tape?" Mattie suggested to me. "It may be getting a little wobbly."

It was. Alan wasn't exactly sure what he was doing, and the tape could have been straighter. I knelt to give him a hand and some instruction, and together, we did a nice, tight job of masking the edges of the baseboard. Then we moved on to the moldings around the windows and doors. Ben opened a can of paint, and Alan and I worked hard to keep from slowing him down.

Toward noon, Ben brought in folding chairs from Mattie's garage, and we pulled them into a circle and helped ourselves to refreshments. Mattie had coffee for the grown-ups and hot chocolate for Alan. Also pastries from the same bakery where I'd gone with Vince's wife, which reminded me of her. This town was small enough that I wondered if Mattie and Carol knew her—but this was no time to ask.

"The paint sure does make a difference!" said Rafe, looking around at our morning's work.

"This will be a great little home for you, Lainie," said Carol.

"Lainie," said Alan, "are you going to live here *all the time*?"

"Except when I'm taking care of you at Mom's," I said. "But *you'll* be here a lot, too."

He didn't look as reassured as I'd hoped.

"Alan," said Mattie. "I have something to show you. It's a surprise."

"Where?" asked Alan, looking around.

"Well, it's in my house," she said. "But you have to promise not to tell Lainie."

He looked a little suspicious for a second, then he nodded.

She set down her coffee and Danish, and led the way to her house, with Alan right behind her. The kitchen door closed after them.

Carol laughed. "Trust Mattie!"

"What's she doing?" I asked.

"I really wouldn't know—except I'll bet your brother comes back feeling a lot better."

She was right. Alan came back with a mysterious, satisfied air, and wouldn't tell me anything about the surprise, not even a hint. But he seemed far less worried and stressed, more a part of the group. For the rest of our time there, I saw him talking casually to everyone, commenting on things, helping wherever he could. He almost seemed taller, as if he'd shot up an inch or two.

I wondered if Mattie had a magic wand in her kitchen. If she did, I hoped she'd teach *me* how to use it, too.

29

Moving consisted of taking a bag of clothes and my tiny hoard of art supplies when I went to pick Alan up at school, and then going to my new place instead of Mom's. No big deal.

Or at least, not until I got there. When I opened the door, I saw how much more work my friends had done since the work party.

Since I'd helped paint the walls white myself, I'd expected the place to turn out sort of blank and bland. Instead, I walked into a room with bright curtains at the windows, still holding some of the sun's light even though it was almost a quarter to four on a January afternoon. The bed in the corner was made up with a patchwork quilt. Near the kitchen, two yellow-painted chairs were pulled up to a light wooden table. Bright pottery and a few slightly battered pots and pans were arranged neatly on the kitchen shelves.

In the opposite corner were two upholstered armchairs, old but clean. On a low table between them was a jigsaw puzzle, partly put together.

As if I'd lived there all along.

I swallowed a couple of times before I found my voice. "Alan! Was this the surprise?"

He smiled and shook his head. "Uh-uh. That's for later."

"So what is it, then?"

"Mattie said not to tell. But she said there'd be a pizza in the freezer. And we're supposed to go to her place after dinner. *Then* we get the surprise."

"But I have to take you home *before* dinner," I said, confused.

"Uh-uh." He grinned at having something to spring on me. "Mom said I can stay over."

"Oh," I said, surprised, and after a second added, "That's *cool*." I also wondered who was staying over at *Mom's*—but I didn't share that.

We settled down in the armchairs. He had a library book in his backpack—something about science for kids. I helped him with a couple of big words. Actually, I wasn't that much above second-grade level myself, when it came to science. It was one of the things I'd figured I wouldn't need, back when I'd had the luxury of taking school or leaving it. But now it seemed kind of interesting.

I worked on the jigsaw puzzle for a while and wondered what Mattie and her friends were planning to teach me. The daylight left the curtains all too soon—in Olympia, the sun went down unbelievably early. I turned on the ceiling light, and the windows sprang back as cold black mirrors. I looked at my dark reflection, wondering if I could paint something like that—a "winter portrait."

I liked the idea, but when we left San Diego, I hadn't been able to smuggle painting supplies in my suitcase, just drawing things. But I could at least do a few sketches. The face should be half-turned, as mine had been when I first caught the reflection, with nothing else clearly reflected and with night outside.

Alan brought me back to reality. "Lainie! It's time for dinner!"

I turned on the oven, figured out the directions on the pizza box, and managed to cook it without burning anything, including myself. In all honesty, this frozen pizza tasted better than the homemade one I'd worked on so hard for Thanksgiving. If I was going to be a housemaid and cook, I had a few things besides science to learn. I decided I'd better go back to the library and check out some cookbooks—at least a basic one—or my employers wouldn't put up with me long.

After the plates were washed, Alan and I knocked on Mattie's back door, and she let us into the kitchen. I could see where the chairs at my table had come from—she had two left at her own table.

She led us into her living room. Piled in the center of the floor were a sleeping bag—old, but nice—a fold-up sleeping pad, a pillow, and a blanket.

"This is for Alan, for sleepovers," she said.

"That was the surprise!" Alan shouted. Before I could suggest that he turn down the volume a little, he ran to Mattie and hugged her. She looked surprised herself, but not like she minded. Not at all.

"I'll get my own breakfast tomorrow," she told me. "I know you have to walk Alan to school. But the next day, I'll expect you in here about seven, and I'll show you what to do."

"Thanks," I said. That wasn't enough, not after all her kindness. "I mean *really*. And the cottage is great!"

"You're welcome," she said.

We lugged Alan's bedding to the cottage and found a good spot for it. When Mattie had gone back, Alan asked, "I don't have to go to sleep yet, do I?"

"No, it's still early," I said. "But remember, you have to get up for school in the morning. Take your shower and get into your pj's—if you remembered to pack some in that backpack of yours."

He rummaged through his pack and pulled out his favorite Superman pajamas. After a shower that drenched the whole bathroom, he put them on and snuggled happily in his new bed, reading his library book.

I pulled my sketchpad out of my bag and started working on my "winter portrait" idea. The face worked out well, but when I stepped back and looked at the picture, the loneliness and blankness beyond the windows was almost too effective. It reminded me that, somewhere out there, people might be looking for us.

I went around to each of my windows and made sure they were locked, then I tested the door, too. Everything seemed secure, but when I thought about it, checking them almost seemed silly. I was pretty sure hardware-store locks and latches wouldn't do much to stop the Mafia.

Alan was watching me over his book. "Are you scared?"

"No," I said quickly. "But it's always a good idea to lock up at night."

I pulled the curtains closed so the windows wouldn't give a view of us, while Alan watched with a troubled expression.

"Are they really still after us?" he asked.

"I doubt it," I said. "Besides, you heard what Mom said. No one who follows the rules has ever been found."

"But what are the rules?" he asked.

"Well, changing our names, moving somewhere else— that kind of thing. We already did all that."

"Oh," he said, seeming satisfied. He went back to his book, and soon dozed off with it covering his face.

Before I turned out the lights, I gently took the book away and laid it on the floor beside his bed. But then I lay awake for a long time and wondered: What else should I do to make us safe? Exactly what *were* the rules?

30

The window was open, the curtain billowing in the breeze. Except the breeze turned the bright print of the curtain to black and white, like an old photo. And then, as the fabric fluttered, the curtain went dark. The pattern of flowers became rippling faces like reflections in black water. I stood and tried to close the window, but faces were outside, too—glass faces like masks, cold and expressionless, with the sky pulsing behind them like it was about to rip open.

I woke up whimpering, and then was startled to see where I was. I looked to see if Alan was awake, but he wasn't. That was a relief. He was already anxious enough.

It was still dark, but when I checked the clock, I saw it was time to get up. Another relief. I couldn't have gone back to sleep after a dream like that.

I pulled myself together, got up, and dressed. Mattie had left us cereal, milk, and bananas for our breakfast, and I got things together and woke Alan up.

"Do I have to go to school?" he asked, still half asleep.

"Yep. It's Tuesday. School, and then I pick you up in the afternoon. Don't you want to tell them about the book you read?"

"Oh." He perked up. "I guess so."

"Then get ready, 'cause we don't have a whole lot of time."

Dressing, breakfast, packing up his things. Before this, it was Mom who had done mornings, so I had to think about every step.

"Did you brush your teeth?" I asked at the last minute, and he had to scamper back and do it. I helped repack his bag, and we set out for school.

It was a longer walk than from Mom's, and I wondered if someday I could afford bikes for us. There were a lot of details and responsibilities, which I didn't mind, but I had to work hard not to miss things.

We had to hurry, but I got him to school on time, and went back to Mattie's to start my first day of work.

I was a little nervous about it, but it wasn't bad at all. In fact, it was more or less the same things I'd been doing at Mom's. I washed her breakfast dishes, made the bed, and did a general cleaning. And all the time, I kept her company—keeping up a flow of conversation that, at least today, included a lot of questions about my past.

I will not lie about myself to these people, I told myself. *If I have to, I'll say I can't talk about something. But no lies— at least, none besides the fake name. That's as far as it goes.*

So I told her about my drawing and painting, and a little about school in San Diego. I was pretty frank about what I did well—art and languages—and what I didn't see any reason to learn—math and science. She wasn't especially shocked to hear me talk like that.

"Just the same," she said, "If you want to be an artist, you need to know all kinds of things. Especially science, because that's the bones of everything—the way objects and animals work, and why they work that way. If I were a painter—which I most definitely am *not*—I'd want to know what lay behind every surface, because I think that would improve my work."

"Did you teach science?" I asked. She sounded like she really enjoyed the subject.

"Oh, not particularly. I taught several middle-school grades. Of course, that's the time when students are starting to get a good idea of their life interests, so it's really exciting to give them the tools they need."

"How did you meet Carol?" It seemed a good idea to keep the subject away from myself, as much as I could.

"I taught her son, Rafe."

She didn't seem inclined to expand on that, so I dropped it.

I made lunch for both of us and cleaned the kitchen. After lunch, she said she wanted a nap. But she asked me to come back after dinner to talk to some of the other teachers who were interested in hiring me, so we could work out a schedule.

So, I was on my own for the early afternoon. I spent some time trying to sketch a scene from the dream I'd had. But the sketch wasn't even close to the image I remembered—I needed paints to capture that. Or maybe it was too complicated. I wasn't sure I could do it at all.

Frustrated, I started off early to Alan's school, and on the way, I remembered I wanted to check the library for cookbooks. That turned out not to take long. But while I was there, Alan's question came back to me—"What are the rules?" So, I decided to see what I could learn about the Witness Protection Program.

I couldn't find anything on the shelves to answer my questions, so I turned to the computers. It didn't take long to find basic stuff about it online. I learned that witnesses in the program had to leave their identities behind and take new names. They were issued new birth certificates and other papers. According to what I read, there was a common misconception that a person would keep their old initials when they changed their name.

A common misconception?

Families would be carefully briefed by federal agents before being taken by car—sometimes changing vehicles along the way—to a new location where they had no connections at all. From then on, they'd be supported with help and advice as they worked out new identities and lives.

Federal agents?

Briefed?

Taken by car?

Supported?

No connections?

I hadn't seen a single federal agent, and no one had told me anything—no one except Mom. I'd been hustled onto Amtrak to get to Olympia by myself. And—according to Vince's wife—Mom had been having an affair with him for a year.

But maybe Paula was wrong? Maybe he'd been having an affair with someone else? And then he and Mom had gotten together after we moved to Olympia?

An idea hit me. I went to the reference desk and asked for an Olympia phone book. Then I leafed through the pages to the end of the *B*'s.

There it was. "Buchanan Vincent," with the address on Columbia and our phone number.

We'd been living in Vince's house all along. And Mom's story about the Witness Protection Program? All a lie.

If the Mafia really was after us, we were on our own.

31

I couldn't tell Alan.

I decided on that even before I got to his school. He'd had so much trouble in his life in the past few months, I hardly recognized him. He'd been so funny and carefree back in San Diego. So bratty. I never would have dreamed I'd miss his little demon act, but now that it was gone, I did. He was easier to deal with now, but I knew it was because he was scared. How could I add to that?

When we got to Mom's, I poured him a glass of juice. We played dominoes, but I was too distracted to be much of a challenge.

"You're letting me win!" he complained.

"No, I'm not," I said. "I'm sorry. I wasn't paying attention. I was wondering where Mom is."

In fact, she was late. I needed to get back in time to meet with Mattie's friends—and before that, I had to confront Mom about her lie.

"When she does get home," I said, "I have to talk to her. It's important, and it won't work if we're both here. I promise not to do this very often, but could you go upstairs when she comes in?"

"This isn't any fun," he said. He had set up a line of dominoes, and now he pushed the first one to make them fall.

"I'm sorry," I said. "I have to work something out with her, and she won't talk to me about it if you're here."

"It's not fair!"

"No," I said, "it's not."

He must have picked up on the tension in my voice. After a few seconds, he nodded. I felt guilty, seeing the troubled look on his face.

"I'm sorry, buddy," I said, and meant it. "I'll pick you up again tomorrow afternoon."

We didn't bother to start another game. Alan waited awkwardly until we heard Mom's key in the door, then bolted upstairs without a word. I heard his bedroom door shut as Mom came into the living room.

"Sorry I'm late!" she called. She didn't sound sorry, or even hurried. "Why was Alan rushing upstairs?"

"Mom, I have to ask you about something."

"What is it?" She sounded more impatient than wary.

I took a deep breath, not knowing whether to expect one of her explosions.

"I know we're not in the Witness Protection Program."

She froze. "Why do you think that?"

There was no way I was going to let her get away with the "Who, me?" act. I'd had enough lies.

"I looked up how they operate," I said. "It's nothing like what we did. For one thing, you knew Vince before we came here, and they don't let you go anywhere you have connections. That's for starters."

Suddenly, she became very interested in taking off her gloves, neatly and precisely, one finger at a time. She pressed them together, folded them in half, and laid them on the table next to the ruined domino game. The glove's fingers splayed out like a fan, and she straightened them again. By the time she had them aligned to her satisfaction, I felt like screaming.

"What makes you say I knew Vince?" she asked.

"Oh, Mom, for goodness' sake. Alan may be seven years old, but I'm not. Someone told me Vince's last name, and I looked him up in the phone book. We're living in his house."

"And exactly why were you checking up on Vince and me?"

"I wasn't," I said. "I don't care *what* you and Vince do. I'm concerned about our safety, so I looked up the Witness Protection Program and how it works. There are a whole lot of other differences, too. There's no way we're in that program."

"You looked up a lot."

Her tone was dangerous, but I didn't care.

"Yeah. Olympia has a library. Books. Computers." I didn't mention it also came furnished with reading tables and Vince's wife. I figured I might need to play that card another time.

She looked at me closely. Then she shrugged.

"Well, you're right. We're not in the Witness Protection Program."

Even already knowing the truth, I was stunned by Mom's admission. I was a prize liar, but Mom? I couldn't remember her ever lying to me in my whole life.

"So why did you say we were?"

"I didn't want you to feel too frightened," she said. "What your dad did was so dangerous for us. I didn't want you to know there was no one protecting us. I still don't want Alan to know."

"But why *didn't* you get us in the program?" I persisted. "If that would have made us safer, I mean."

"It was too late," she said. "You know how things work with the government—one delay after another. The people I talked to wouldn't even let me know if we qualified. We had to get away immediately."

"There's nothing in the news about Dad's trial," I said.

"There's no trial," she said. "Not for your Dad, anyway. I told you, he pleaded guilty. He made a plea bargain in exchange for information about the others. You have to assume they know that. Or they'll find out soon enough. How long it could be before we're targeted, I have no idea. Maybe nothing has happened yet. Maybe they've given up. Maybe not."

She spoke very seriously. It gave me chills.

"So, what it means is that nothing has changed," she said. "I know you've been careful. Well, *stay* careful. That's all I can tell you."

She went to the window and looked out at the darkening afternoon. "You'd better get on home. The sun will be down before long."

I walked home as fast as I could. I'd talked to Mom too long, and now I'd be late to Mattie's meeting, if I didn't hurry.

But even as I pushed myself to get there, I tried to clear my mind. It wasn't going to be easy to put aside what Mom had said. But I had to look normal when I talked to Mattie's friends. No matter how badly they needed a housemaid, they wouldn't want one who was being tracked by the Mafia.

That didn't exactly square with my stand as Angel of Truth, and I knew it. I'd just have to keep an eye out for trouble, take care of Alan, and make sure nothing bad happened to Mattie and her friends for trusting me.

A few months ago, I hadn't had any real responsibilities. Now the list got longer every day.

32

Winter kept pelting us with endless storms. The drumming rain never let up.

After weeks of it, I was ready to scream. But if I believed what I read in the newspaper, I was the only one. Almost everyone else seemed breathless with anticipation. Would we break the record for the number of rain days? Or would the sun come out at the last minute and spoil everything?

I didn't get it. The most rain days in a row, ever—who would want that? Was it sort of a souvenir thing, like a T-shirt? *I SURVIVED THE OLYMPIA DELUGE.* Or bragging rights that we'd really suffered?

I'd have been happy to give up the bragging rights, if I could just see the sun. The dreary weather got me down. Mattie and my other clients seemed to do OK, though.

I was incredibly busy. I cleaned and cooked for them, re-minded them of appointments, kept them company. And did just about everything else they needed, too.

When the weekends came, I was worn out. So, I wasn't too pleased on a Saturday afternoon in late February, just when I'd made a sandwich for my lunch, when a knock at my door turned out to be Rafe.

To tell the truth, I didn't much like him. Still, I thought Carol might need something, so I asked him in. He left his umbrella on my tiny porch and followed me inside.

"Is something wrong with your mom?" I asked.

"No," he said. "Everything's fine."

"So, what's up?"

"Remember Mom's friend Ben who came the day of the work party?"

"Sure."

"He has a sailboat down in the harbor. He and Mom were tossing around the idea of a day sail, and Mom was wondering if you'd like to join us."

I was nicely surprised by the invitation. "I think I'd like to, but I don't know anything about sailing."

"They don't need help with the boat," he said. "They just thought you might like to come along."

"When?"

"Tomorrow, if it doesn't rain. Otherwise, we'll try again next Sunday."

"I *would* like to. Thanks."

I waited for him to make his exit. But he just stood awkwardly in the middle of my one room. I realized it had been nice of him to come out in the rain and invite me. I wouldn't have expected anyone to go to that much trouble.

"Sorry about not having a phone," I said. "And thanks for coming over to ask me."

"No problem."

Another awkward pause, and I soldiered up to the job of hostess. "Would you like a cup of tea or a sandwich?"

"Tea would be good."

"I'll fix us some," I said.

He sat at the table, watching quietly as I put a pan of water on the stove to boil. While we waited, I took the other chair and nibbled at my sandwich, wondering why he'd wanted to stay.

"How are you getting on with choosing a college?" I asked, for want of something better to say.

He sort of drew in, as if I'd brought up something painful.

"I don't know," he said. "I'm not sure I even want to go on with it. Here's Mom, pushing me to choose a graduate school, and I'm thinking about dropping out."

"Why?" I asked. I'd quit high school, of course, but I hadn't had a choice.

He didn't answer.

"I'm not looking for a chance to put you down," I said. "What's the problem?"

"Well, you know my dad died," he said cautiously.

"I did hear that," I said.

"He had Alzheimer's."

"I'm sorry. That must have been hard."

He looked like he wasn't sure what to say. "It's not that, exactly. Mom is driving me nuts."

"How?"

He looked around the cottage almost longingly. "You wouldn't understand. Here you have your own place, you can do whatever you want. There's no one breathing down your neck every minute, telling you what to do."

I decided not to mention I was busier than anyone ought to be, and one of my parents was a criminal, and the other couldn't care less about her kids. Instead I asked, "Like, telling you what?"

The pan was boiling furiously by now, steaming up the windows. When I'd poured water into two cups, I passed him one along with a cardboard box of tea bags and a spoon. We sat quietly, stirring our cups, watching the water turn into tea.

Finally, he said, "Dad was an engineer. Sounds good, right? But if I'd lived his life, I'd have wanted to die, too. He worked his butt off, and he almost never got to be himself. In the end, it's like he forgot who he was. Forgetting who *we* were, and everything else, was almost a detail."

"Well, but what . . ."

"So, Mom wants me to finish college and do something like engineering. Or politics. Or medicine. One of those professions that eats you alive."

"What do *you* want to do?"

"I don't want to be an engineer or a politician, for sure."

"I don't mean what *profession* you'd choose. What do you want to *do*?"

He considered the idea for long enough that I wondered if he'd ever looked at it quite that way before.

"I want to make a difference," he said. "I know it sounds corny, but I've always wanted to make things better somehow. But not if I have to turn into someone else to do it."

"How could you turn into someone else if you were doing exactly what you wanted?"

He shrugged and took a few sips of tea. "So, are you taking your own advice? What do *you* want to do?"

"Paint," I said. "Or maybe make prints. Art, anyway."

"If that's what you want, why are you working as a housekeeper?"

"It started out because I needed a job," I said. "And art is still what I most want to do. But I like taking care of people, too. I'd like to have more time for art, but right now, I'm pretty much doing what I want."

"I don't think I want anything that clearly." He sounded so bleak.

Leaving his cup half full, he stood and pushed his chair back. "Thanks for the tea. I'll have to think about what you said. About tomorrow—Mom said to meet her at the office."

As I saw him out, I had an idea.

"Maybe you could get clearer about what you want by looking at other people," I said. "Like, whose life could you see yourself living? And then, what would you have to do to live like that?"

He nodded and lifted his hand in a short good-bye. Then he opened his umbrella and walked off toward home.

Somehow, the rain seemed to suit him. But now that I knew more about him, I sort of understood.

33

The boat trip did have to be postponed for a week, but the weather forecast for the last Sunday in February was for clear, breezy weather. It was chilly, and I thought it might be even colder in the boat, so I wore my warmest clothes and hoped for the best.

I walked to Carol's office early in the morning. The empty streets made me nervous—I felt so exposed. If the Mafia was looking for me, they wouldn't have to pick me out of a crowd. Not in Olympia, especially at that hour.

But were they even looking? I had no idea, and there was no one to ask. Not Carol, or Mattie, or my other clients—that would be the end of my job. The police? They'd think I was nuts.

I kept telling myself not to be so dramatic, not to get paranoid. It was easy to say. If I believed Mom, anyone I saw could be a hit man—even though everyone turned out to be just another person minding their own business. And every sound could be someone coming to kidnap Alan and me—only, it was always a cat in the bushes, a truck engine starting, a kid on a skateboard.

That was it—*if I believed Mom*. In the past, I'd never doubted her word. Now, I didn't know what to think.

She'd covered up her affair with Vince, and she'd told us this weird story about being in the Witness Protection Program. She'd said that was just to keep us from worrying, and

I couldn't see any other reason for her to come up with it. If she'd just wanted to leave Dad, once he was in jail, there was nothing to stop her.

I turned it over and over in my mind, but it seemed like she *must* be telling the truth about the Mafia, outlandish as it sounded.

Maybe I *was* going nuts. I felt anxious all the time, like I used to feel the morning before a math test. My stomach hurt, too.

And this sailboat trip today—I was just hoping it wouldn't be a disaster. What if I got seasick? On the other hand, I'd seen sailboats in San Diego Bay all my life, and wondered what it would be like to be on one. And this was the first really fun thing I'd had a chance to do in months.

For the past few weeks, I'd cleaned houses, cooked meals, run errands, tended gardens, and taken care of my brother. I'd studied at night—and those old teachers were no pushovers. I'd probably learned more in those weeks than I normally did in a year.

Of course, it all felt satisfying, even if it was hard. And there was one really bright spot: They'd just found me an art teacher—a volunteer, thank goodness, so at least I wouldn't have to scrub his bathroom. If that worked out, maybe this whole crazy turn my life had taken would turn out to be what I really needed.

If only Alan and I were safe. I'd never been much for prayer, but now I found myself trying to contact whoever or whatever was in charge—if anyone was.

Let us be safe . . .

I reached Carol's office as she was unlocking the door.

"Want to use the bathroom before we go?" she asked.

"Doesn't the boat have one?"

"Well . . . yes. Sort of. The head on a boat isn't quite the same as a normal bathroom."

I was taken aback. "What's the difference?" I asked.

"The main one is that a boat is pretty tight quarters, so you may not have as much privacy as you're used to. At least the head on North Star has a door—some boats just have a curtain. But it's a pretty thin door. Also, you can't flush the paper, because everything goes into a holding tank."

"Oh." I couldn't think what else to say.

"You never sailed before, right?"

"Right," I said. "I hope I don't get seasick."

Carol smiled. "It shouldn't be rough. You don't usually get motion-sick, do you? You didn't say anything about it on the train."

"No."

"Just don't drink much of anything. Let me know if you feel queasy. Ben has crystallized ginger in the galley in case someone feels sick." She laughed. "Sometimes I snitch some because I just like it."

"Ginger? For seasickness?"

"Oh, yes. It works quite well. And it doesn't make you drowsy like seasickness pills, either."

That was reassuring.

We took turns using the bathroom and then headed down to Percival Landing, where Ben had his boat. He was on the boardwalk, waiting for us.

As we chatted, I couldn't help thinking that Ben didn't match the stereotype of a sea captain. Tall, thin, gray-haired, he looked like a lawyer, not a sailor. Which, in fact, is exactly what he now told me he was: a lawyer for family court.

"What's that?" I asked.

"Adoptions, on a good day," he said.

"What about on bad ones?"

He grimaced. "Custody. Domestic violence. All the family nightmares. I try to stay out of those, unless someone really needs help. Which, God knows, happens often enough."

"That sounds hard," I said.

"It is. But it's like picking up the garbage—someone has to do it."

"I don't know how you stand it. I just do housework, so I clean up messes, too, but I think I'd rather have my kind of mess than yours."

"Frankly, I'm not so sure I wouldn't prefer that myself," he said. "But Carol says you do a lot more than that. She says you're kind of a lifeline for the people you work for."

I glanced at Carol in surprise.

"Well, it's true," she said. "Don't undervalue what you're doing for your people. *They* certainly don't."

She turned to Ben. "It's really another part of the problem you deal with. Families aren't doing what they used to. It takes so little to keep most old people in their homes—just someone who looks in every day, keeps the place clean, maybe balances a checkbook or picks up a few groceries. It used to be taken for granted that younger family members would take care of it. Now they live probably a thousand miles away—or if they're local, they just can't be bothered."

She laughed. "Uh-oh. Same old soapbox. Cut it out," she chided herself, smacking her left hand with her right.

Ben laughed, too. "It's a good soapbox," he said. "But soapboxes are for land. Today, we're on the boat. Free as dolphins." He looked lovingly at North Star.

When I'd first heard about Ben's boat, I'd figured it was a rich man's plaything. When I'd learned more, I thought of it as a quirky, inconvenient home for him. But now I had a flash of understanding: Ben could stand his horrid but necessary job because he was connected to the city only by a couple of ropes. No matter how bad his day, when he came home at the end of it, he could lie down in freedom.

I thought about my own work. It wasn't horrid at all—in fact, it made me feel good. Everyone's dire warnings about diapers hadn't come true, and I knew that, if I did have to do that sort of thing, I wouldn't mind. As Ben put it, someone had to.

I wondered, was I truly a lifeline? I could see I was making a big difference for at least a couple of my people. It wasn't that they lived in fear of death, as far as I could see. But they did dread having to go to nursing homes. Even delaying that was worth a lot.

But where was the freedom to end *my* day? I had nothing in my life that compared to North Star.

Not yet.

34

My thoughts were interrupted by Rafe joining us. "Am I late?" he asked.

"Nope," said Ben. "Right on time. Let's get going."

Ben let us in a gate, and we went down a wooden walkway that connected to the dock.

"Wow!" I said. "This is way too steep!"

"Low tide," Carol said. "The dock floats, you know. As the tide goes out, the dock drops lower, so the walkway slants more."

I hadn't known—hadn't thought about it—but it made sense. I just hoped the tide would be a lot higher when we came back.

We filed along the dock till we came to Ben's boat. It was big for a sailboat—but I knew Ben lived on it, and if I thought of it as a home, it seemed pretty small.

It was so graceful, though. I couldn't stop looking at it. It reminded me of the "tall ships"—the big, old-fashioned wooden sailboats—that I'd seen once from a distance when they sailed past San Diego. Most of the boats around us didn't even look like they belonged in the water—they sat on it uneasily, like buckets bobbing up and down. North Star was different somehow. Sleek, as if it could fly.

Rafe climbed quickly onto the boat. Carol collected all the bags and jackets we'd brought with us and handed them up to him. Then she followed, sure-footed as a cat. The boat rocked, and I felt nervous about trying to get on. Helplessly, I looked to Ben for guidance.

"Just get a good grip and don't hesitate," he said. "The boat can shift when you're in mid-step, so you have to move decisively. Don't ever put your arm or leg between the boat and the dock."

Rafe reached a hand to me, and I made it without much trouble. Ben climbed aboard last.

Ben started with a short list of rules and other "need-to-know" stuff. I was surprised when he passed me a life jacket.

"I can swim," I said.

"That's good," he answered. "But wear it anyway. Puget Sound is so cold, you may not be able to swim as well as you think. Where are you from?"

"San Diego," I said, before I remembered not to give out personal information.

He shook his head. "The water down there is a whole different story. If you capsize in San Diego Bay, you probably just get a fun swim. Here, you can die of hypothermia in just a few minutes."

I looked at the water with something between respect and fear. Even the morning sparkle on the calm marina seemed to be a frosting of light over glassy faces like the ones I'd dreamed. I shuddered.

"A boat this size is very unlikely to capsize," Ben said, "but watch your footing, and don't forget to hold on to something if you move around the deck. Carol says you've never sailed before, right?"

"Right," I said, a little shakily.

"Just watch this time, then," he said. "Next time we go out, I'll show you the ropes."

It was a good thing they didn't expect me to be much help. Besides my not having the slightest idea how, there was just too much to look at.

The sails were still bundled tightly. Running his motor, Ben steered the boat slowly through the crowded marina while Carol and Rafe arranged our bags and coats down in the cabin. As we came into more open water, Ben turned the boat slightly, and Carol and Rafe raised the sails.

The sails hung limp for a second, then fluttered like flags. And then, as Ben turned the boat, they caught the wind and went taut, gently curved.

It was one of the most beautiful things I'd ever seen.

Somehow, as the sails filled with wind, pulling the skimming boat, I felt gladness go through me, with no idea why. Though no faces appeared in the sails as they had in the fluttering curtains of my dream, I could have put them there. Only, these faces would have looked toward a destination, hopeful and strong.

Ben, busy as he was with the boat, glanced my way and seemed to understand my feelings. He nodded briefly at me, but said nothing.

I looked straight up the mast, blinking at the sun. And I imagined sailing straight from the sound into the sky, past the clouds, backwards against the turning of the earth, back in time. The Mafia would turn into seaweed, stringy kelp, and I'd fly above it all, fly away. Sail back to last summer, sail back to being Linda.

A sweet idea, and it soothed me for a few minutes. Then I realized what that would mean. Go back to my old high school, to all of my old life? Give up my new friends? Leave my people needing someone to take care of them? Never live in my cottage? Give up my new connection to my brother? Never have this day?

To lose so much would be as bad as anything the Mafia could do. And if fear made me willing to lose it, I'd deserve to.

I turned back to watching my friends work the boat. Seated slightly out of the way, I began to make sense of what they were doing, and I wondered if they'd teach me. Mostly, I wished I'd brought my sketchpad, and I drank in the sights, memorizing them for later.

When noon came, Ben brought North Star a little closer to shore, and we stopped for a while. He and Carol spread lunch on the table in the cabin, and we sat on built-in benches around it, helping ourselves to sandwiches and coffee.

"So, what do you think?" Ben asked me.

I shook my head. "I haven't gotten to the 'think' part yet. I'm still just being astonished."

Once again came that quick nod that said he understood.

35

The thing I liked best about my job was that I'd become more than a maid to Mattie and my four other clients. It was true that none of them could pay me even as much as a maid should make, but I got by pretty well, especially since I wasn't paying rent at Mattie's.

When I was in their houses, they were the boss. In a way, anyhow. But to me, they were really halfway between teachers and grandparents. It was fun to talk with them and find out about their lives.

I didn't even mind learning math, since Mr. Lorbear was teaching me. He could make it interesting at least, and sometimes even fun. And Mattie made me see the connection between my art and the science I had to learn. Mrs. Clemens was very pleased with my English skills. Also, she'd really gone out of her way to find me an art teacher. Susan Evans and Miss Allbright, my other clients, were just as good. I liked them all—a lot.

I wished I could be more open with them—tell them my real name and what I was doing there. I wished I didn't have to worry about bringing danger to them, which bothered me a lot every time Mom got going about the Mafia again. I tried not to think about it, but I felt guilty, like I was some kind of Trojan horse.

I checked the computers in the library about once a week to see if anything was going on with the illegal immigrant case. There was nothing at all, not the slightest mention, in any of the newspapers I could find online. I sort of hoped Dad had changed his mind about testifying—that way, his partners in crime might leave us alone. And then I felt guilty for that, too, because what they'd done was horrible, and they'd do it again if no one stopped them.

Sometimes I hated him. And Mom, too, for that matter. Alan and the old people were my family.

So, the day after the sailboat trip, I was brimming over with fun things to tell my clients, and looking forward to hearing what they had to say. I wondered if some of them had sailed, too. Maybe they could give me tips.

I let myself in Mattie's back door on the dot of seven, as usual.

"So, how was it?" she said. "Did you get seasick?"

"Not at all, " I said. "It was beautiful! I wish I'd brought my sketching things."

"Well, if that boyfriend of Carol's gets any idea you might crew for him, you can count on being asked again."

"Is Ben her boyfriend?" I asked, surprised. I knew they were friends, of course, but I hadn't had an idea there was any romance between them.

"Hmmm. Maybe you should ask her," she said. "Of course, she hasn't been a widow for very long. But you never know."

She gave me a tucked-in little smile that told me she would say no more but also drew me in as a confidante. I had to smile back. Mattie was a lot of fun.

I got her breakfast and tidied up a little. Then I went to Mrs. Clemens's house.

I let myself in the back, with my eye on a clump of dandelions that seemed to have sprouted overnight—or over the weekend, anyway. Mrs. Clemens wasn't in her usual chair in the kitchen, waiting for breakfast. I thought she might be in the bathroom, so I sliced her grapefruit and put two pieces of raisin bread in the toaster. But when it was done, she still hadn't appeared. Puzzled, I checked the bathroom, but it was empty, the door wide open.

I found her in the living room, hunched over in a chair, a blanket around her shoulders. I knelt on the floor, right in her line of vision.

"Are you OK?" I said softly.

She shook her head. Her face was pale and sweaty. She seemed to be having trouble breathing, let alone giving me much information.

I squeezed her hand and stood up. "I'm getting help," I said.

She gestured with one hand, but I had no idea if that meant yes or no, and I wasn't willing to argue about it anyway. I went back to the kitchen and called 911. If that wasn't OK with her, I guessed she'd just have to fire me.

I didn't have long to worry about it. The paramedics came with an incredible amount of noise and bustle. While they turned her living room into an ER, one of them took me into the kitchen and asked me for information. But aside from her name and age, there was nothing I could tell him.

Almost before I knew it, I was standing alone in the house, listening to the ambulance wail dwindle as she got farther from me and closer to someone who could help.

I walked around her place, automatically straightening things—Lainie, the housekeeping robot. I put the grapefruit half in the refrigerator and covered it with plastic wrap so it wouldn't dry out. I threw the toast in the garbage and washed the plate. I shook the crumbs from the toaster and sponged off the counters.

The bed was tossed and tumbled, as if she'd had a horrible night. I stripped the sweaty sheets off it, turned the mattress, and made it up with fresh sheets and pillowcases from the linen closet. She had a beautiful old quilt with stars all over it, and I laid it on top and smoothed out every wrinkle.

"She'll be back soon," I said out loud. "She'll be back really soon. She'll want things fresh and nice."

That made tears come to my eyes, so I shut up. Talking to myself in an empty house seemed kind of crazy anyway.

In the living room, the paramedics had left a real mess—all kinds of medical trash. Also pieces of her nightgown, roughly hacked up. I looked at them numbly. Then I got the trash can from the kitchen and stuffed it all in, arranging the contents to bury the things the paramedics had left, just as Mom had buried and hidden the wrappings of her prepared foods when we first moved to Olympia. That seemed like another life—one where people could worry about things like that.

I picked up the blanket from the living room floor and folded it. The edges were crooked, so I took it into the bedroom and refolded it on the bed, checking the binding to make sure there weren't any worn spots for me to mend. It was OK, so I carried it carefully to the linen closet and arranged it neatly on a shelf.

I thought I'd better lock up before I left, so I made the rounds of the house, closing and fastening windows. I had no idea where she kept her keys, but her purse was on her dresser. Feeling horrible, I scrabbled through it, trying not to touch anything I didn't have to. The keys were there.

The front door was already locked, and I took care of the back door as I left. The dandelions seemed to smirk at me as I fled without pulling them up.

The only thing I could think of was to run back to Mattie. As I burst into her living room, she looked up from a book she was reading, surprised to see me when I wasn't due back until dinnertime.

I opened my mouth but nothing came out. She gaped in astonishment as I collapsed on a leather hassock and cried and cried.

36

When I picked up Alan from school that afternoon, I was still feeling pretty shaky. He didn't notice at first, wrapped up in telling excitedly of a play his class was giving, and of how he'd been cast as one of three princes. I wasn't sure what the princes did, but it must have been something important.

Before long, though, he stopped and eyed me accusingly.

"You're not listening!" he complained.

"Yes, I am. You're going to be a prince in the play. That's really good." I tried to make my voice happy, but it sounded hollow even to me.

"You don't sound like you're glad about it."

"I will be when I see you," I said. "I just couldn't imagine it yet."

"Why?"

I sighed. "I'm not feeling too good right now. Mrs. Clemens got sick this morning."

"Did you catch it?" he asked.

"No, it's not that kind of sick," I said. "I think she had a heart attack. I had to call the paramedics."

"Did she die?"

"I don't think so."

"Then she'll be OK?"

"I don't know," I said.

That was the end of the conversation. We trudged up Fourth Avenue for a few more blocks, and then turned north. Alan liked to run and play in a vacant lot that was right at the tip of East Bay. There was a tiny stream running through it, with stepping stones, and he'd worked out all kinds of games and fantasies about getting across. But today he barely broke stride.

"I wish I could have gone with you on that boat," he said, looking over the bay.

"We didn't sail over here," I said. "I think it's too shallow. Sailboats never come down near this end."

"I still wish I could have gone."

"Maybe next time. I'll ask."

We left the water behind and slogged up the hill toward my place. I felt like my shoes were made out of lead, and Alan didn't seem to have any more energy than I did.

When we got to the cottage, I poured him a glass of juice and another for myself. Sitting at the table, we sipped from our glasses and avoided each other's eyes.

Finally, he burst out, "Is Dad gonna die?"

"Of course not," I said. "Why did you think that?"

"There was this show on TV. This guy was in prison. He was on Death Row."

"Dad's not on Death Row," I said, hoping that was true. Surely *that* would have been in the news.

"But he's in prison," he insisted.

"Right. But most people in prison are only there for a while. Then they let them out."

"When are they letting Dad out?"

"I don't know. I don't think they've decided yet."

"I miss him."

Mostly, I didn't. Mostly, I was just angry with him and disgusted by what he'd done. On the other hand, Alan was seven years old. He didn't need me to ruin his memories of Dad.

"He'll be back someday," I said. What we'd do then, I didn't know.

"Lainie . . . what did he do?"

I hesitated. "Did you ask Mom? She'd know more than I do."

"She just told me she couldn't talk about it. What did he *do*? Did he kill someone?"

"No," I said quickly. "He just did something with money that he shouldn't have done." Something that made a bunch of people die—but I left that part out.

"Oh. Did he steal some money?"

"No," I said. "It's a business thing."

"I don't get it."

He wasn't going to let go of the subject until he *did* understand something, so I stumbled on.

"When you have a business . . . there's stuff you can do, and there's stuff you *can't* do. I mean, there's laws about it."

"And you go to *prison* if you don't do business right?"

"Well . . . you *can*."

He thought about that for a while.

"Lainie?"

"Uh-huh?"

"When am *I* gonna die?"

"Not for a long time, buddy," I said. "Mrs. Clemens is really old. She's ninety-one." I did a little math in my head. "You won't be ninety-one until 2089. So, don't worry about it."

"Oh."

He looked a little reassured, and I let him think it over in peace. Some of the stuff he was working on was too big to crack. We sat silently for what seemed a long time.

There was a tap at the door, and Mattie came in.

"Well, it looks like she'll pull through this time," she said. "It was good you got there when you did."

That made me feel a little better, but not much.

"Was it a heart attack?"

"The early stages of one," Mattie said. "I spent most of the day at the hospital. She doesn't have any kin, so I'm the one she designated to handle things for her if she ever needed it."

"Did you see her?" I asked.

"Just for a few minutes this afternoon. She was better. She said to thank you."

"What hospital is she in?"

"St. Peter's," Mattie said. "Stupid name," she added irritably, pushing her glasses to the top of her head and rubbing her eyes with the heels of both hands. "Why would anyone name a hospital for the keeper of the Pearly Gates?"

"Will she be OK?"

Mattie pushed her glasses back into place and set her mouth in a thin line. "Lainie, no one knows. She's over ninety, and she's had a heart attack. She could have another one at any time. She may never be able to come home."

"But she doesn't want to go to a nursing home!"

"Who does? But there's no way she can afford in-home nursing care, either. She may not have a choice."

"I'll take care of her! I won't charge any more than I am now!" I knew how childish I sounded, but I couldn't help it.

"That's sweet of you, dear, but you're not a nurse. You and I could help, of course, if she gets stronger. But if she doesn't . . ." Mattie trailed off. "Anyway, you can feel good about this morning. You probably saved her life."

Alan had been listening quietly to the conversation, but now he burst in. "Lainie! You saved her life! Could you save Dad?"

He put his hand over his mouth and looked from one of us to the other, realizing he'd slipped up.

Mattie didn't comment, but her sharp look told me she wouldn't forget, either.

37

Mattie went to visit Mrs. Clemens every day, and I often went with her when I could spare the time. At first she was so weak and tired, we could only visit for a few minutes.

When she was stronger, they moved her to another part of the hospital, a kind of rehab place. She stayed there for a couple of months, at least. It was easier to visit her there—we could stay longer, and the hours were more flexible.

It made a big difference to me to be able to go with Mattie in the evening after work. I'd tell Mrs. Clemens about the neighborhood, or read to her a little—she couldn't pay attention for long. If we came after they'd brought her dinner tray, Mattie would try to get her to eat something, but it was never very much.

Mrs. Clemens was determined to go home and talked about it every day. It made me sad. I didn't see how she could, even if I did spend more time caring for her. Like Mattie said, I wasn't a nurse. And I had my other clients, too, so I couldn't spend that much time with any one of them, no matter how much she needed me. As for Mattie, for all her gutsiness, she wasn't strong enough to help Mrs. Clemens the way the nurses did. And we were all she had.

So, I was surprised one evening when Mrs. Clemens greeted us with a big smile. "They're letting me go home tomorrow!" she announced. "Can you pick me up?"

"Of course," said Mattie. "When?"

"Noon, they said. Of course, if that's not convenient . . ."

"It's fine," Mattie said firmly. "I'll be here. But will you have a home care nurse?"

"Yes, the hospital worked it out."

She seemed a bit vague about it, and still very tired. We didn't stay long.

"I hope this won't be too much more of a burden on you," Mattie said as she drove us home.

"I don't mind," I said. "I just hope she really can do it. I don't think she looks a lot better."

"I don't, either," said Mattie.

It turned out we were right. Early the next morning, Mattie got a call. Mrs. Clemens had passed away during the night.

Mattie told me when I came at seven to fix her breakfast.

"She was happy," I said, when I could speak. "At least she was happy. She thought she was coming home today."

Mattie nodded.

"She wanted to be cremated, so I'll take care of that," she said. "She didn't go to church anymore—said the churches had all changed so much, it was like a whole different religion. So, she didn't want a funeral."

Mattie sighed. "I'll call her lawyer this morning. There's a lot of paperwork, I guess. She told me she'd left what she had to me—mostly the house. I'll have to get it in shape and sell it. No way I could pay the taxes on two places, and I don't want to start getting into rental property. I'm too old."

She looked at me. "You were a real friend to her, Lainie. I know she appreciated it."

"Should I tell the others?" I asked. "They all knew her, didn't they?"

"Yes, I guess you should," Mattie said, sounding depressed. "Tell them I'll call them later."

I went to work at the other houses, burdened with my sad news. As I passed Mrs. Clemens's backyard, I saw the patch of dandelions, now flourishing in defiant triumph. I had an impulse to dig them up right then. It really made me mad that they were still alive and Mrs. Clemens wasn't.

I had other things to do, though, so I kept going. Cleaning the houses was the easy part. I had to tell three people that their friend was gone. Not unexpected, I knew, but that didn't matter. Gone was gone, and who would be next?

I usually felt happy just seeing the flowers and trees in the yards next to my alley. Apple trees were everywhere. The blossoms had fallen and small green apples were beginning to swell on their branches. Only, now I was wondering how I would feel if there was a good chance I wouldn't be around next year to see it.

Maybe that was something I couldn't know. Maybe my elderly friends had learned something, *had* something—philosophy, religion, courage, or just weariness—that made the prospect of leaving the world more acceptable than I'd expect it to be.

But then there was Alan. What could I do about *his* big questions? They were hard enough to handle at *my* age. How much harder was it for him?

"What about the Mafia?"

"Are they really still after us?"

"When am I gonna die?"

I wasn't much of a mother figure, I thought. None of what I'd said could have been very reassuring.

"They're probably back in California."

"Not for a long time, buddy. Don't worry about it."

I was just heading him off to hide my own lack of answers. And Mom was worse. She hardly talked to him at all, except to yell at him.

If we didn't do more than this, didn't do *better* than this, he was going to grow up completely twisted. I could already see the strain getting to him, and it wasn't fun to watch.

For a moment, I thought about trying to get Mom to change, but that was hopeless. *Worse* than hopeless. When I'd moved out, Vince had more or less moved in. Alan spent more and more weekends at my place, and from what he said, he mostly hid in his room while at Mom's.

It wasn't that Vince hit him or anything—I'd questioned Alan closely to make sure. But Vince was big and loud and sarcastic, and he didn't like kids. And Mom was so besotted with him, she didn't even notice that Alan was withering like a plant she couldn't be bothered to water.

I had to do *something* to get my brother back to normal. But I didn't think I could do it alone, and I didn't see how anyone I knew could help. There was Mattie, but first she would need to know what was going on, and I couldn't risk losing my clients by telling her. Carol, ditto. And Paula, Vince's wife . . . Well, what could she do that wouldn't make things worse?

Ben. A lawyer for family court.

"What's that?"

"Adoptions, on a good day."

"What about on bad ones?"

"Custody. Domestic violence. All the family nightmares."

If this wasn't a family nightmare, I didn't know what was. Maybe Ben was the one I should talk to.

But how could I know if he really was a good guy? Lawyers could be crooks—I'd seen it on the news more times than I could count. Maybe I could trust him, maybe not. If it was just me, I'd take the chance. But I couldn't gamble with Alan.

Rafe couldn't help. He wasn't much older than *me*.

Well, but . . . It worked the other way, too. If Rafe didn't have much power, he also wasn't much of a threat. And even if he couldn't offer a lot, he could at least tell me if he thought I could trust Ben.

Of course, if I told him about the Mafia, he might think I was crazy. Or he might tell Carol and get me fired. But then, he wasn't on the best terms with her. That was too bad in one way, but it also told me he could act on his own and not be some kind of puppet.

I could start with sailing. Get in touch with him and see if he could lend me books about it or something. Try to get to know him, see what he was like. Figure out where to go from there.

He might think I was putting the make on him, which could be a problem. But compared to the Mafia, that was not a big deal.

I'd reached Mr. Lorbear's house. Time to cook, and clean, and try to pay attention in my math lesson. And time to start telling the bad news.

For a moment, I just stared at his door, feeling completely discouraged. Then I remembered: There was work to do, and people who needed me.

I turned the knob and went in.

38

When I called Rafe and asked him to teach me about sailing, he hesitated for a moment and then said, "Sure. No problem." Then he added, "I don't have a boat, though."

I settled into one of Mom's—or, I guess, Vince's and Paula's—living-room chairs and pulled the phone onto my lap. Phoning from Mom's place made me feel like a kid again, especially since Rafe was living at *his* mom's, too. But this was the only place to make a call.

"Well, I know that," I said. "But there's a lot just *about* boats I need to learn, so I'll know what people are even talking about. It makes me feel really dumb. It's like a whole different language."

He laughed. "Sort of. I guess I hadn't thought too much about it, since I've been sailing since I was little."

"Did you go with your mom?"

"Her and Ben. Dad didn't sail. He said he got seasick, but honestly, I think he just didn't want to go."

"That's a beautiful boat Ben has."

"It is," he said. "It's a gaff-rigged cutter."

I laughed. "See? There you go. Foreign language."

"Hmmm. I can see how you might need a translator. Want to walk around the marina on Sunday and get a lesson in Boat?"

"Sure," I said.

"Percival Landing boardwalk at Fourth Avenue? Ten o'clock?"

I agreed, and we finished the conversation with filler like "Say hi to Carol for me," and "See you soon."

I sat and thought a while after we hung up. Now that I'd
gotten to know him better, I'd actually started to like Rafe. Yes,
he could be rude sometimes, but not because he really meant
to be. He was just going through a hard time and wasn't good
with people. At least he was real and honest.

And I'd seen a different side of him now—on his visit to
my place, and on the boat. Maybe a little too serious, and a
little jumpy, but a nice guy. And kind of vulnerable.

Still, I wanted to steer clear of flirting with him. At least
for now, my interest in him was strictly practical.

If I could get some kind of line on Ben from him, that
would help a lot. And even if I couldn't, it would be good to
have someone to talk to. That was the worst thing about Mom's
harping on the theme that anyone could be a bad guy—it made
me so isolated. I had to solve everything by myself, and it was
not possible. A friend would be a big relief.

At the same time, I didn't want to lead Rafe on. It wouldn't
be right to use him.

I had to laugh at myself at that point. Who did I think I
was, a supermodel? My present glamour budget was nil, and
I looked it—clean, but definitely shabby. *And* with a seven-
year-old boy in tow, most of the time. Like a couple of street
kids. At least I was too young for anyone who could subtract to
mistake me for Alan's mother. Just the same, he didn't exactly
enhance my romantic potential.

Vulnerable wouldn't be enough. A guy would have to be
desperate to be interested in me. And Rafe probably had a
girlfriend already, anyway. Most nice guys did.

I sighed, thinking about Nicholas in San Diego. At least a
hundred times, I'd thought of phoning him. Mom's paranoid

warnings had stopped me again and again. Lots of people had seen Nicholas and me together. So, maybe his phone had been bugged. How could I be sure it wasn't?

Anyway, I had a plan. It was slow and indirect, but it was the best I could come up with.

I checked the clock. Mom was on time more often, now that Vince had moved in. Surprised at how late it was, I went upstairs to Alan's room.

I tapped at the door, but he didn't answer. This wasn't unusual—he'd taken to sitting on his bed most of the time he was at Mom's, as if he were under some kind of room arrest. I stuck my head around the door.

"Hey, buddy," I began.

"Hey," he said listlessly.

I let myself in and shut the door. "Things are pretty lousy, right?" I could think of more descriptive words than *lousy*, but I tried not to use that kind of language around my brother.

"Yeah." He moved his feet for me to sit on the end of the bed.

"Listen," I said. "I'm working on a plan."

"What." It wasn't a question, just a minimal response. How much more could this kid take?

"When I went sailing the other day, I met a man named Ben. I guess he's Carol's boyfriend. Anyway, he's a friend of hers."

"So?"

"He's a lawyer. I'm going to start by finding out if he's OK to talk to. If he is, I'll get him to help us."

He looked more interested. I didn't know how much I could expect a seven-year-old to know about lawyers, but Alan was pretty smart. He'd probably understand a little more than most kids his age.

"How are you going to find out?" he asked.

"I'll start by asking other people about him. You know, people who've known him a long time."

"Maybe they won't know if he's a bad guy."

"He probably hasn't exactly announced it, if he is. But if he is a bad guy, there'll be other ways to tell."

"Like what?"

"Well, I can ask other people what he does. Who he knows, that kind of thing. If he's some kind of fat cat, with a lot of flashy friends, I'd be more worried about him than if he just does his job and hangs out with people like Carol."

"Oh." He didn't sound convinced.

"And," I said, developing the idea as I went along, "I guess I could find out about his job. He works in family court. He does divorces and adoptions, that kind of thing. Maybe I could find out who he works for. I mean, *whose* divorces and adoptions he does."

He thought about it for a while. Then his eyes filled and tears started rolling down his face. He didn't make a sound, but they just kept coming.

"What's wrong, buddy?" I asked. "Did I scare you?"

"No!" he yelled. "I'm not scared of bad guys! *Vince* is a bad guy! And I have to live with him!" He started sobbing and couldn't talk about it anymore.

I didn't tell him that being kidnapped by the Mafia would be a lot worse than living with Vince. Because in the long run, maybe it wouldn't.

39
Rafe

After Lainie's call, I sat there in my room and looked around. The place was trashed.

Not trashed as in "Clean-up-your-room-Rafe-it-looks-like-a-pigsty." Trashed, meaning wrecked. Totaled.

Mom and Dad had been pretty generous in letting me buy what I wanted for my room. And Mom was good about privacy, meaning she hadn't been through the door in a long time. Well, she'd have a cow when she *did* see it. I'd scrubbed my oak desk with bleach so many times, it looked unfinished. Same for the bed. And the dresser.

The good news was, they still matched. The bad news was, it was because they were all ruined.

The carpet and bedspread, too. There were white spots all over them. The room smelled like a public swimming pool, a chlorine reek that stayed in the back of my throat all the time.

There was more. I hadn't been to class in weeks. It was kind of funny that Mom was sweating what kind of high-powered career I could have. Forget graduate school—I wasn't going to get through my sophomore year. I didn't even have the energy to ask my teachers to let me make up the work. I was going to crash and burn.

I'd never had a lot of friends, but since leaving high school, I was down to zero. I barely remembered when I'd last had a date.

The kids I'd graduated with were gone. I couldn't think of one who'd stayed in Olympia.

I'd chosen the local community college because of Dad's illness. I was going to be the hero son and take care of Mom. Then I'd blown that, too.

Worst of all, my whole life had turned into something I didn't even recognize. I imagined germs crawling on everything, all the time. My hands were raw from washing. I could barely manage to leave the house, because as soon as I got out of the shower, I felt dirty like I needed to shower again.

I couldn't touch food in restaurants, or even at home unless I made it myself. I'd taken a cup of tea from Lainie because it was boiled water and ought to be safe—then I'd barely been able to touch it anyway. If she knew how crazy I was, she'd run away screaming.

And she was the only person I'd met in the past year I even liked. Fine, sounds good, I met a girl I liked. She wants me to teach her about boats. Nice opening. Just Lainie and me, prowling around Percival Landing.

What then? How could I ask her or any other girl to date me? The idea of holding hands made me nearly panic. Forget doing anything more. A girl might appreciate that a guy wasn't pushy about being physical, but sooner or later she'd expect . . . *something*.

I'd blown school, my relationship with Mom, friends, girl-friends, everything. I couldn't stand the way I was living. With other people, I could still keep up a pretty good front. But I had to face it. I was out of control.

It looked like there was no choice but a shrink. At least I didn't have to go to Mom and do a mea culpa. The school had a counseling service. I had no idea how much help they could give me, but I could start there.

40

Lainie

I got to Percival Landing early on Sunday. Fourth Avenue was quiet, so the bench at the corner was perfect for watching the marina and daydreaming. I had more time for that, though, than I expected. Rafe was almost twenty minutes late.

I heard running footsteps and turned to look. It was Rafe, looking stressed out.

"Sorry I'm late," he said.

He didn't offer any excuse, but we had all day. It was no big deal. I picked up my sketchpad and backpack.

"Let's walk," I said, "and you can tell me about the boats."

We headed along the boardwalk, past a statue of a couple of middle-aged people kissing. It made me think of Mom and Vince, and I shook my head, like a dog shaking off a fly.

Rafe pointed out different kinds of boats and riggings. A few boats I saw sitting near each other didn't look like they were built to move at all. They were more like houses in the water.

He noticed me looking at them. "Those houseboats are really nice ones," he said. "Did you want to draw them?"

"Not right now," I said. "I'm mostly interested in sailboats."

"Of course, you know Ben's a liveaboard," he said, as we continued down the boardwalk. "But most sailboats are just used for recreation. And at that, a lot of owners don't take them out much. We may not see any today actually going anywhere."

"Why not?" I asked, surprised. "I think I'd sail every chance I got, if I had one."

"People think they will, but it doesn't happen," he said. "For one thing, Olympia doesn't get a lot of wind."

"That could be a problem," I agreed.

"And then . . . I don't know. People just don't. Even on good days, the marina's full of boats. The wind's fine, it's sunny and beautiful—but there the boats stay. Who knows?"

"At least Ben *lives* on his," I said. "So, he gets *that* use out of it."

"True."

"It's not much space. Does he have a house or anything besides?"

"No. But he has his own office, so I guess he can store things there. Maybe he even has a place there to sleep, if it's really cold or stormy."

"What does he do, exactly?"

I hoped I wasn't pushing it with my interest in Ben. But Rafe didn't seem suspicious.

"Family law. Adoptions, mostly, I think. He doesn't like divorces, I know that. Still, I think some of his cases get pretty messy. I'd hate to get involved with stuff like that, myself. But Ben says his job is to help straighten things out."

That didn't sound anything like a Mafioso. But I decided to leave off the inquiry for now. There was so much to see! We passed some people flying kites in a park next to the boardwalk. If I'd been on my own, I would have stopped and made a sketch.

"Speaking of Ben," Rafe said, "he's not down here today. But he said we could go down to his dock, if you wanted another look at North Star."

"Oh, good," I said. "I'd really like to draw a picture of the sails."

"They'll be stowed," he said, sounding surprised. "You only hoist them when you go out."

That made me feel dumb, because I'd watched them put away the sails myself. But he didn't make a big deal of his superior knowledge. I liked that.

When we got to the right gate for Ben's boat, Rafe pressed the combination numbers and we headed down the ramp, or bridge, or whatever it was called. It wasn't as steep this time, so the tide must have been higher.

When we reached North Star, I sat on the dock. The boards were beginning to warm up in the sun, so it was a lazy, comfortable place to sit. Rafe didn't sit, though. He sort of squatted, looking uncomfortable. I wondered why, since he wasn't wearing particularly good clothes. It made me a little nervous, like we shouldn't stay too long.

So, I sketched quickly, and he looked over my shoulder and pointed out the names of things. I knew *mast, deck,* and *bow* of course, and some others that I'd heard here and there. But *sheets* was a funny name for ropes. I'd have thought that would be for sails. Then there was *forestay* and *halyard* and a dozen more. My head was spinning.

When I was done, he looked hard at the drawing. "That's *good,*" he said. "If you did paintings or prints, you could sell them in one of the galleries."

"I wish," I said.

"Well, why not?"

One big reason was I couldn't afford painting supplies, let alone things for printmaking. I wasn't about to say that, though.

"Oh . . . I don't think I'm ready. I meant to go to art school this year, but I didn't get to. Mrs. Clemens gave me the phone number of an art teacher. I'll probably give him a call."

Much as I wanted to do that, I kept putting it off. I didn't understand why, either. I felt sort of paralyzed about it.

"You'd better," he said. "If you don't, she might haunt you."

I was shocked, and I guess I looked it.

"I'm sorry," he said. "She and Mom were friends from before I can remember, and I liked her a lot. I didn't mean to be rude or disrespectful or anything. But I knew her pretty well, and I can tell you for sure—if she found you a teacher, the last thing she'd have wanted is for you to drop the ball."

He took another look at my drawing. "Plus, you're really good. And you don't want to clean houses *all* your life, do you?"

41

"Just coffee this morning," said Mattie when I came in at seven.

"No breakfast?"

"I'm not hungry."

I looked at her carefully to see if she was sick. She seemed OK—maybe like she'd had a bad night, but nothing serious.

"Are you all right?" I asked.

"I'm fine," she said, dismissing my concern with unusual brusqueness. "I've been thinking. It's about time you started doing practice tests for your GED."

"Oh. I hadn't thought about it," I said. I was a little preoccupied with the coffeepot. The filter wouldn't seat right, and I was sure it would run over as soon as I turned it on.

"Check the library for test prep books," she said. "Some will be on the reference shelves to use only in the library, but there will probably also be a few you can check out."

"OK," I said.

What Mattie didn't realize was that I didn't have a library card and couldn't get one. No ID. Now that Mom had admitted we weren't in the Witness Protection Program, I knew that any ID card she might have for me as Lainie Foster would be a fake, and probably a bad one. Most likely, she didn't even have one.

"There are also courses to prepare you for the test," Mattie said. "But they're not cheap, and anyway, I doubt you need one. You've had some catching up to do in science and math, but you've done very well. It shouldn't be that long before you're ready to take the test."

It suddenly occurred to me that I'd need ID to take the test. No way were they going to let me in without it.

"You turn nineteen in December, right?" Mattie asked.

"Right. Does that matter?"

"You have to be nineteen to take it, unless . . . well, unless a lot of things that wouldn't apply in your case." She made a dismissive gesture with her hand, as if shooing the "other things" off the table. "But you should still get ready now so you can take it as soon as you're eligible. It's not an easy test."

"OK," I said again.

The coffeepot went through its sputtering finale, and I poured a cup and passed it to her.

"Another thing," she said. "I have to get Violet's house ready for sale, and I'm thinking you and Rafe might be able to do it for me."

Violet? Oh, Mrs. Clemens.

"I never did construction or anything like that," I said carefully, wondering how she could imagine I might have.

She laughed. "It's mostly cleaning and painting the interior. I know you'd do well. Rafe, too. Might as well keep it among friends, so to speak. Would you like the job?"

I wanted the money, definitely. I needed it for art supplies. I'd be starting my art lessons in a few days. Well, *probably* I would. I'd be meeting with the art teacher, anyway, and I was fairly confident he'd take me on. Also, working on the house would give me a chance to talk to Rafe without seeming to chase him.

"I think so," I said. "But what's your schedule? If you're in a rush, I'm not sure I could fit it in."

"There's no big hurry. As long as it doesn't get bogged down, I won't crack a whip. I'll see if Rafe's interested, too.

And by the way, I was Violet's only heir, so she left me all the contents of the house as well. If there's anything over there that would make your place more comfortable, feel free to claim it. I'll be calling the Children's Hospital thrift shop to take away the rest."

"Well, thanks," I said. "But don't you want any of it?"

She shook her head. "I have too much stuff already. I may give some of my *own* clutter to the thrift shop. And as far as 'something to remember her by,' I remember her very well without it. I always will."

She sipped her coffee and turned toward the window. I concentrated on rubbing an imaginary spill off the stove, to give her time to get collected. After a while, she turned to me again.

"Her keys are on the rack by my front door. You might as well go ahead and get started. Keep track of your time— it'll come out of the estate. If you find any papers, bring them to me. You can pack things for the thrift store as you clean. Get boxes from the grocery store, if they still give them out, or else I'll buy some. And of course, you can put linens and clothes in trash bags."

She looked seriously upset. I understood, or thought I did. The idea of dumping an old friend's possessions into trash bags was pretty brutal.

I touched her arm. "Don't worry," I said. "I'll take care of it. If anything unexpected comes up, I'll ask you what to do. Aside from that, I'll just let you know when to call for the pickup."

Mattie pulled a wadded tissue out of her sweater pocket and blew her nose.

"You're a good girl, Lainie," she said. "I wish . . ." She blew her nose again and didn't finish the sentence.

I wondered what she'd meant to say. And for the rest of that day, I found myself trying out different endings.

"*I wish Violet hadn't died.*"

"*I wish I didn't have this inheritance to deal with.*"

"*I wish I knew who you are.*"

42

I entered by the back door, as I always had. In the kitchen, I stopped to take a deep breath and calm myself. For some reason, my heart was racing.

A week had passed since Mattie had asked me to get the house ready to sell, a week I'd mostly dragged my feet about that and everything else. It was hard even to get up in the morning, let alone do anything. I knew I was just putting in time at my clients' houses, giving nothing but the minimum. I'd talked to the art teacher once, promised to come by with samples of my work, and left him hanging.

I just felt down, but I knew there wasn't any slack in my world for me to bug out of things. And feeling *ashamed* about how I felt didn't give me energy to do better. It felt like one of those nightmares where you can barely move.

Mrs. Clemens's house was as eerily silent as the day they'd taken her to the hospital. No ticking clocks, nothing. It was a long time before I could begin.

I pulled a trash bag from a box in the lowest kitchen drawer, opened it, and started on the refrigerator. It was pretty bad—I should have taken care of it weeks ago. The grapefruit I'd cut for her that last morning was covered with white mold beneath its layer of plastic wrap. I gagged as I threw it in the bag, and tears came to my eyes.

It was so unfair—not to me, to Mrs. Clemens. Life was so unfair. I didn't know how anyone could stand it.

Then a kind of fury came over me. I pulled food off the shelves, everything in the refrigerator and freezer, spoiled or not. I dumped or poured it all into the bag, barely looking at it. I saved the containers, or most of them, piling them in the sink to wash later.

When there was nothing left in the cold white box but dull wire shelves, I stopped as if I'd been slapped. Panting a little, I closed the refrigerator door and sat down hard in one of the kitchen chairs.

What would Mrs. Clemens have thought, to see me acting like a nut case? How would Mattie do this job, if it was hers? Would Mattie act like some drama queen, slamming things around and moaning about how awful everything was?

"OK, Linda," I said to myself. I didn't answer, so I started over. "OK, Lainie." That sounded better, so I went on. "Take this bag of garbage out and throw it in the can. And throw your stupid ideas in with it, while you're there."

I didn't mention out loud what those stupid ideas were, but I knew: the *no-fair* notions that kids have. The idea that everything is supposed to be happily sorted out in thirty minutes, minus commercials. The idea that everyone is entitled to an ideal life, and if the world doesn't provide that, then someone needs to be blamed, big time.

I hauled out the heavy bag and threw it away. On the way back in, I was stopped by the sight of the dandelion patch. By now it had bright yellow flowers.

"Screw it," I said.

Leaving the dandelions alone, I went back inside.

Now I cleaned the kitchen carefully, as I had so many times. Stovetop, oven, counters. Dishes, cabinets, table. It was like any other day I'd been there—making it clean and nice.

Then came the hard part. If I could keep my mind off the reason for this being done, it would just be like helping someone move.

First the cabinets—I started with food. I knew Mattie didn't want it, and even though I could probably have used some of it, neither did I. So I sorted what she had—opened or unopened packages. The unopened could go to the food bank. Opened ones went into another garbage bag. I hated the waste, but it was the best I could do.

Next, I worked on the other cabinets and drawers. I started two sets of boxes—one for the thrift store, another for myself. I could use a few pans, dishes, kitchen towels, things like that. I packed everything carefully, using newspapers from the recycling bin in the laundry room.

I felt calmer. It really *was* like moving, or even just spring-cleaning. Or the time in San Diego I'd helped Mom paint the cabinets. Mrs. Clemens's kitchen was cluttered with boxes, but it didn't look so bad. Not morbid or scary—nothing like that.

Since I felt better, I decided to start on the living room right away. But just inside the door, I stopped short. The room was exactly as it had been when the paramedics left with Mrs. Clemens. The light slanted through the curtains just the way it had that morning. Everything was the same, except she was gone.

"All right," I said. I needed my sketchpad from back at the cottage. I turned around and left to go get it.

A couple of hours or so later, back in Mrs. Clemens's living room, I propped my drawings against the couch and stepped back for a look.

The first drawing showed Mrs. Clemens as she'd been on that day, with the blanket around her shoulders. I'd always had a knack for drawing from memory, and now Mrs. Clemens rose from the paper in all her pain, in all her hope that she wasn't facing the end, in all her fear that she was.

Another memory portrait: Alan, as he'd looked in San Diego the morning we saved the bird—mischievous as an elf, a mirror in his hand. But behind him, I'd set an unknown figure, possibly menacing, possibly just a parent come to tell him to get ready for school.

Another: North Star, sails straining in the breeze, with the strong, hopeful faces I'd wanted to place in them, gazing forward.

And the last, a self-portrait: Lainie with a mask held close to her face. The mask—expressionless but identical to the face—a portrait of Linda Farley.

Leaving the drawings on the couch, I took my empty boxes and trash bags into the bedroom. I went through all the drawers, hoping she hadn't left anything private like diaries or old love letters. Thankfully, all I found there was clothes for the thrift-shop bags.

Books on the shelves went into big boxes, and knickknacks were carefully wrapped and fitted into small boxes of their own—all for the children's hospital. When I'd finished, I pushed all the bags and boxes together into one corner.

I'd decided not to keep anything for myself but the beautiful starry quilt. Tucking it under one arm, I gathered my drawings and sketchbook under the other.

I had everything I needed.

43

Not knowing where to look, I studied the pattern of Brian Shaw's living-room rug while he considered my drawings. For an art teacher, he certainly had an ugly rug. Maybe he never looked down.

"Interesting," he said.

If that was all he could come up with, I didn't think he'd be much of a teacher for me. I waited.

He cleared his throat. "I can definitely work with you. But there's always a point where you need practice more than instruction. You may be nearing that point, at least with your drawing. Do you paint?"

"I have," I said. "I don't have any materials now."

"Why not?"

"It's sort of a long story," I said. "My parents split up, and my mother moved us up here from California. I moved out of her place when I turned eighteen, and I'm cleaning houses for a living now. There's not a lot of money for art supplies."

"I see."

He thought for a few minutes, while I went back to analyzing the rug.

"I take it you'd be interested in a better job if you could get one."

I shook my head. "No, not really."

He gave me a blank stare, and I tried to explain. "It's not exactly true that I just clean houses. That's kind of a simplification, really. I clean, but I also take care of a group of old people. I like them. I wouldn't want to quit. I like them a lot."

"But if you don't have enough money to buy the supplies you need . . ."

"I probably wouldn't have any more if I quit my job. It doesn't pay a lot, but I have a free place to live. If I had to pay rent, I honestly don't think I'd be ahead."

"What about scholarships?"

"I didn't graduate from high school. I'm going to take my GED early next year, though."

He looked back at my drawings. "Your work is salable. Had you thought about that?"

"How do you sell a drawing?" I asked. "I've never done it."

"Do you want to sell these?"

It occurred to me that if I was supposed to be in hiding, selling portraits of Alan and me might not be too smart. And I wasn't ready yet to sell a picture of Mrs. Clemens's last day in her house, if I ever would be.

"The boat one, maybe," I said. "The others are sort of, well, personal."

"I can show it to a gallery for you," he said. "And you can do more, if you'd like. But pencil drawings by an unknown artist aren't likely to fetch much. Here's an idea. Why don't I give you painting supplies to get you started? Or whatever you'd like to work with. You can pay me back later, when you get some sales."

"That's really generous," I said in surprise. "But what if my work doesn't sell?"

He shrugged. "*C'est la vie.* But somehow, I'm pretty sure it will."

Later that day, I met Rafe at Mrs. Clemens's house to get an idea of what we still needed to do. The bags and boxes and almost all the furniture were gone. I'd held back only a couple of wooden chairs, in case I needed to climb on something or sit down for a while. They made the place look even more forlorn than if it had been completely bare.

Rafe seemed more relaxed than I'd ever seen him. He looked around the place, noting where we needed to scrub the walls before we painted, and what carpet needed replacing. At first I thought he didn't care much about Mrs. Clemens, but then I remembered what he'd said earlier—how he'd known her for years.

"Doesn't it bother you to do this?" I asked.

"Not really," he said. "But if it bothers *you* a lot, I'm sure Mattie would understand if we waited till later. She's not that impatient to sell the house."

"No," I said. "I think it would be worse to have it sit empty. But I mind that I didn't have more time to get to know Mrs. Clemens."

"I know what you mean about that," he said. "But she appreciated how well you took care of her. So do all the others. Mattie's always talking about what a good job you do."

He hesitated. "You know, after Dad died, I decided . . . No one lives forever, but if you can keep your mind till the end . . . Well, that's about all you can ask."

This had suddenly turned into sharing time. I took a deep breath. It would be so easy not to go on, not to say more. And everything I'd lived with in the past ten months shrieked at me to stop, to not tell. But on the other side of that equation were Alan's misery and my own growing inertia and slipping into depression. And wanting to be able to finish school, to go to art school if I chose, to draw what I wanted and sell what I wanted.

A new thought flashed into my mind: As hard as it was to trust my friends, it made more sense than trusting Mom. I was devastated by what she had become. Before we moved to Olympia, she'd seemed to care about Alan and me. Now she seemed only selfish and indifferent, to the point of shamelessly lying to us.

Standing there in Mrs. Clemens's house, I remembered how *she'd* been. She'd known all along I had secrets, and she'd respected them. As Mattie did, and Carol, too. How could I have worried that any of them would hurt me?

Mrs. Clemens was gone. The house was empty, swept clean. Now it was time to sweep out the old lies. I should have done it while she was still alive.

"I lost my dad, too," I began. "In a way."

"You mean he died?" said Rafe. "Or your parents divorced, or what?"

"He's in prison."

"Ouch. What for?"

"Money laundering. He had something to do with illegal immigrants—laundering money for the Mafia. They all died, all the people in the truck. They suffocated, and he got caught." It came out really garbled, but I figured he'd get the general idea.

"Oh, shit," he said.

"I was wondering about Ben," I said. "Mom's gotten so weird, and it's not fair to Alan. I thought Ben might give me some advice. Do you think so?"

"I'm sure he would," said Rafe. "But right now, he's on his way up the coast. He does that every year—takes North Star on a cruise to Alaska. He'll probably be gone all summer."

I stared at him, stunned. Fall seemed like a year away—almost like another kind of time, unreachable from here.

I'd dithered and dallied, and now it was too late.

44

I must have looked on the point of collapse, because Rafe took my arm and guided me to one of the lonely-looking chairs, then sat in the other.

"How can Ben just take off like that?" I asked. "What about his law practice?"

"He has partners. Sometimes he docks North Star and flies back, if something important comes up. I guess he schedules his work so he doesn't have too much to do for a while."

"Oh, *shit*," I said.

"What exactly is going on?" he asked. "Can you go back and explain it one piece at a time?"

"Dad got involved with an illegal immigration ring," I said, trying to spell it out clearly. "He was laundering money for them. A bunch of people suffocated in a truck in the desert, and he went to prison."

"Where?"

"You mean where did it happen, or what prison?"

"Either. Both. Do you have the details? Where was the trial? Have you seen him?"

I shook my head. "I don't know much at all. The part with the immigrants was on the news. There was no trial, because he pled guilty. We left San Diego the day after Mom told me."

"Why?"

"Mom said he was going to give evidence to the state or the federal prosecutor or someone, and the Mafia would be after us.

First she said we were in the Witness Protection Program, but later she admitted we're not."

"So what happened about the Mafia?"

"I have no idea."

"Hang on a minute," he said. "I'm trying to put this together."

He closed his eyes for a minute, while I wondered what he could possibly be thinking.

"OK, one thing," he said finally, looking at me again. "Ben has email on North Star. We can get him if we have to. But first let's just think for ourselves."

He hesitated. "Let me fill you in on a couple of things. When Dad died, I sort of fell apart. I didn't realize it was something no one could have prevented."

"You mean, you blamed yourself?"

"Yeah, I did. More or less. And I got a ton of other crazy ideas. I thought he might have gotten sick because of something in the water, something he ate, a germ. I didn't know.

"Anyway, I was afraid I'd get it, too. I ended up washing all the time—showering over and over, washing my hands till they bled. I couldn't do chores like take out the garbage—too dirty— so I left everything for Mom. And I counted things, arranged things in neat patterns."

"But what does that have to do with my dad?" I asked. I was sorry about his troubles, of course, but I couldn't take them on, not right now. I was overwhelmed by my own.

"I'm getting there," he said. "By the time I talked to the counselor at school, things were out of control. I was using so much water, Mom asked if I was running a meth lab in my room. That's how out of touch we were."

"Did the counselor help?" I asked politely. I still didn't understand why he would bring this up right now.

"It was a start. It helps just to have a name for it—*obsessive-compulsive disorder,* that's what it's called. I'm not out of the woods yet, though, not by a long shot.

"But I only started telling you all this because of one of the things we're doing in therapy. It's kind of a *what-if* exercise. You know, like, *what if* touching a doorknob without washing your hands *doesn't* make you sick. That kind of thing. It's like you challenge yourself to find out. See what I mean?"

To me, he just seemed wrapped up in his own ideas. "I still don't see—"

"Wait, I'm coming to it now. Let's try it on your problem. Your mom hasn't been truthful with you, agreed?"

"Right, but—"

He put up a hand. "In the therapy I'm doing, we work on the difference between delusions and reality. But lies are a lot like delusions. So, why wouldn't the same method work on your mom's BS? We don't really know how much of what she says is true and how much is lie. So, let's look at that."

"OK," I said, wondering what I was getting into.

"Let's start with the Mafia. What if they're *not* after you?"

This was getting silly. "I don't know why Mom would lie to me about *that.*"

"Don't worry about *why,* just go with the idea. What if they're not?"

I sighed. "Then I guess I could stop being scared and start doing whatever I want. But if they're not after us now, Mom said they *would* be as soon as Dad testifies."

"Here's another *what-if:* What if he never testifies?"

"Then I guess they'll never try to get us. But how could I know? I tried to find out. I looked on the Internet, and I couldn't find anything *about* Dad."

He looked at me sharply. "You looked, and you didn't find anything. So . . . what if there was nothing to find?"

"What do you mean?" I said, confused.

"What if he's not testifying because he's not in prison?"

"Why wouldn't he be in prison? He did something horrible!"

"What if he didn't?"

"If he didn't, then why would Mom *say* he did?"

"Don't *worry* about why," he said again. "You looked on the Internet, and you didn't find anything about your dad's arrest, right?"

"Right," I said, wondering if he was brilliant or crazy.

"Nothing about a trial, right?"

"Right."

"Nothing about testimony, right?"

"Right."

He leaned forward, elbows on knees, and looked directly in my eyes. "What if it never happened?" he said. "What if your dad's part in that immigrant tragedy was just something your mom made up to get you to leave with her? What if you went back to San Diego and found out for yourself?"

I stared at him in shock, trying to take in what he'd suggested. I tried to talk but only sputtered.

"What if I went back to . . . What if I . . ."

What if?

45
Linda

I stood outside our house in San Diego, wearing the backpack I'd brought with me on the Greyhound. I felt so nervous, I thought I might throw up. But I'd never forgive myself if I chickened out. So, I walked up the path and rang the doorbell.

After a short wait, the door opened, and I stared into the face of Dad's secretary, Shelley. Both of us gasped at about the same second, as if on cue.

She was wearing a bathrobe.

"Who is it?" called Dad's voice from the breakfast room.

Shelley stood aside and let me in. When Dad saw me, he jumped up from his chair.

"My *God*, Linda! *Where have you been?*"

I didn't know what to say. I opened my mouth and shut it again.

"Let's go in the living room," Dad suggested.

I dropped my backpack and sat on the couch, with Dad and Shelley facing me in armchairs. Less than a year ago, I'd sat in that same spot while Mom told me her—told me her *what*, exactly? Was the whole thing some huge scam?

What should I say? Who should I believe?

"OK, Linda," said Dad. "Here we are. Now, talk to me, please!"

"Dad," I said, "when you went away—"

"Went away?" he yelped. "When *I* went away? *You're* the one who disappeared!"

"Last fall," I said, bewildered. "You went away last fall. And didn't come back."

"I went to Indonesia," Dad said. "You *knew* where I was, and you knew for how long. I talked about it for weeks! When I returned, all of you were gone. I had the police searching for you, for God's sake."

I looked at him stupidly. "You weren't arrested?" *What if?*

"Why would anyone arrest *me*?" he asked.

"Mom said you were laundering money."

Dad looked at me like I'd lost my mind. "She said *what*?"

So, I told him the whole thing. The threat of the Mafia. Mom telling us we were in the Witness Protection Program. Our flight from San Diego. Mom living with someone else. Everything—maybe a little jumbled, but more or less coherent.

Well, *almost* everything. I didn't tell him where we lived, or our new names. Ten months of hiding had made me paranoid.

"This boyfriend of Mom's—I'm sure she knew him before," I said. "So, did she do all of that because of him?" I looked at Shelley, sitting motionless as a doll in the chair where Mom used to sit. "Or was there another reason?"

"God-*damn* it!" Dad yelled.

"Stop, Bill," Shelley said. "Let's give her the truth, OK?"

She turned to me. "Yes, your dad and I were having an affair. And your mom found out. They hadn't gotten along for quite a while, and he was pretty sure she was involved with someone, too. I figured there'd just be a divorce. Then your Dad went to Indonesia—"

"And came home to an empty house," said Dad bitterly. "On top of that, the bank accounts had been cleaned out, almost to nothing."

Well, that answered one *why*.

"So, she told you I was in *prison*," he said. "And kept you from asking questions by inventing a Mafia bogeyman who would get you if you rocked the boat." His voice was rising. "And she kidnapped you and Andy. Goddamn it! I'll have *her* arrested—see how she feels about that!"

I'd known he'd be mad, for sure, but I hadn't expected anything like this. Would he really drag the family through that kind of hell? I had to do something to cool him off right now, before things got out of hand. But what could I do?

I found myself wondering what *Mattie* would do.

Mattie. I'd watched her again and again, persuading people to do what was best. Persuading Alan that it was more fun to be a grown-up and help us paint my cottage than to sulk like a little kid. Persuading me that I should learn science because it was part of art.

If only I could think what she'd say to Dad. But I'd never seen her deal with a rage case like this. I played for time, thinking as fast as I could.

"Well, I don't know what you mean by *kidnapped*." I said. "I mean, she is our mother."

He shot me the kind of look George Washington might have turned on Benedict Arnold.

"Spousal kidnapping—it's still kidnapping, Linda. How do you think I felt when I came home and found all of you gone? What was I supposed to do? Just rearrange my stuff, be glad I got the whole closet now, and go on from there?"

"But—"

He charged on, ignoring me. "She changed your names and did a bunk with you. What'd she do, dress you all up like some kind of goddamn spies so no one would recognize you?"

A vision of Mom in her trailer-trash getup flitted across my mind. Dad had her number, at least about her being a selfish drama queen. But what about him? He sure was playing the Ken that matched her Barbie. The way he was acting now, they were the perfect couple. *Mattie, what in hell do I do?*

"But, Dad," I said, "these are just legal things. It's not a kidnapping like she held us for ransom."

"Ransom?!" Dad exploded, jumping out of his chair. "No, she took the damn ransom money, too! She erased our joint accounts like . . . like a mugger who gets your debit card! I'm going to clean *her* clock, so *you* need to tell me where she *is,* and *right now!*"

I was legally an adult. I could walk away from my father, and I would if I had to. I'd already given up Mom. But—talk about kidnapping—Alan was hostage to both of them. If they didn't stop all this, right now, Alan's future could only be a mess.

That's what Mattie would make him see. Because that's what mattered.

I wished I could yell at Dad or shake him to make him see. But I had to be careful, or I would hurt Dad too much for him to understand. My words could come across as a pouncing tiger for him to fend off, or else as a kitten he could invite into his lap. My choice.

So, I kept my voice down. "Hang on a minute, Dad. You need to think about Andy. He's in bad shape. I mean it. He's seven years old, and he's getting into a real depression from everything he's been through. I'm asking you, *please,* don't make things worse for him."

That pulled him up short. He sat back down. "So what do you want me to do?" he asked, still angry but quieter. "I don't imagine you dropped by just to say hi. I've been robbed, and you're telling me to accept it? I may have my daughter back, but I still don't have my son. Are you telling me to wave bye-bye?"

"No," I said, "I don't expect that. I *want* you to get him back. Maybe you can get back some of the money, too. If you let Mom know you're on to her, you'll have her cold. Threaten her with legal action if you have to. But no arrests. No police. No *revenge.* If you don't promise that, I won't tell you where they are."

He looked taken aback. I'd made him see his real choice.

"All *right,*" he said. "Let's hear more of what you have in mind. If it's a decent plan, I'll go along."

"Have your lawyer get in touch with her and cut some kind of deal. Or if you think your lawyer can't do it, confront her yourself. I can give you the phone number of her boyfriend's wife, if you need backup evidence. Between the two of you, I don't see what kind of argument Mom could make. Besides, she doesn't even *want* Andy. I bet she'll send him back to you in a minute."

"What about you?" he asked.

"I'm eighteen," I said. "I have a life of my own. I have a cottage, and friends, and teachers, and a job. I'm even going to be selling my work in an art gallery. I'm staying where I am."

"While Andy comes here," he said, musing.

"He needs a parent," I said, "and it sure isn't going to be Mom. But I hope you'll let him visit me sometimes. We've gotten pretty close."

"Jesus," said Dad.

He sat quietly for a while. Shelley went to him and knelt by his chair. She took his hand, and when he didn't respond right away, she pulled it gently and made him look at her.

"She's right," she said.

I used to really like her, I thought. *She seemed so nice, and— I don't know—maybe she is. I guess none of this is her fault, really. Why couldn't my stupid parents just get a divorce, like other people?*

"Dad," I said softly, "you can end up with both your kids as friends. Or you can screw up Andy's life completely, whether or not you ever find him again."

"And lose my daughter," he finished for me.

I didn't answer. Two minus two leaves zero. Math wasn't my best subject, but even I could do that one.

Dad was silent for what seemed a long time. Finally, he seemed to relax a little. "OK, Linda. You win."

"I don't think we have any winners," I told him. "But this is the only way to get past it."

"I agree," Shelley said. "We all need to get on with our lives. We weren't exactly blameless, either, Bill. Anyway, we have to put Andy first. Get him back, and we'll take care of him. Get some of the money back, too, if you can—but if you can't, it's not that important. Let it go."

"What about you, Linda?" said Dad. "Aren't you planning to go to college?"

I drew a deep breath. There was no Mafia. I didn't have to be someone else anymore. I could go to art school now, if I wanted. But what *did* I want? Did an artist even need to go to college?

I looked around the room. Being there brought back that last morning of my old life. Whatever I decided, I'd be fine, like Mom's baby bird. I was ready for flight—ready to be on my own.

"Maybe art school," I told Dad. "I don't know, right now. If I decide to go later, will you still help with tuition and things?"

"Of course," he said.

"Do you still have all the stuff I left behind? Can I take my art supplies back with me?"

"Of course you can. We can ship things to you, too."

His voice had steadied. He sounded like himself now. I was shaky with relief, but I couldn't collapse just yet. I had a few more things to take care of.

"Can I stay here tonight?" I asked. "We still have lots to talk about. And I can't get a bus back home till tomorrow."

"Why don't you stay a few days," he said, "and let me buy you an airline ticket back? Can you take off from your job that long?"

"I think so, if I call and let them know." I looked at Shelley. It was her house, too, now. "Is it OK with you?"

She gave me a warm smile. "Sure. Your room is pretty much as you left it. Make yourself comfortable."

"Thanks," I said, standing up. "Is it OK if I go for a walk? I'll be back in less than an hour, I think. I just want to look up a friend of mine."

They actually looked relieved, which gave me the giggles all the way to Nicholas's house. I imagined them doing a sweep of the place. Clearing Shelley's clothes out of my room. Taking her birth-control pills out of the medicine cabinet.

Well, birth control or not, she was about to be mother to a boy of seven, nearly eight. She'd be *my* stepmother, too. And she'd probably do fine.

I wasn't sure what I'd say to Nicholas. Except I wanted him to know what happened, and I had to be the one to tell him.

He'd have just graduated from high school now, and I had no idea what he planned for college. I doubted he'd be interested in going to school in Olympia, and besides, we hadn't had time to get that close. Most likely, he had another girlfriend.

Then there was Rafe. Crazy-like-a-fox Rafe, with his *what-ifs*. He'd said he still had a lot of work to do in his therapy, and I had to agree. I couldn't see any relationship with him beyond friendship, not for a long time. If ever.

But I was only eighteen. There was plenty of time before I needed to think about that kind of future. With Nicholas, or Rafe, or anyone.

I rounded the corner of Nicholas's block. Just by dumb luck, he was in his front yard, bent over. Gardening? Tying his shoes? When he straightened up, he caught sight of me coming down the sidewalk. He froze right there, standing like a player in a game of statues.

I didn't hesitate. I walked up and touched him on the cheek.

"Are you going out with anyone?" I asked.

46

In a small airport terminal like the one I arrived in at Sea-Tac, a group the size of my welcoming committee looked like a mob. Well, maybe that wasn't the best word, under the circumstances. Like a crowd, or a throng. Something good to see.

As I got near them, Alan broke free of Mattie's hand and hit me like a torpedo.

"You came back!" he shouted. "You came back!"

I bent down and hugged him. "Of course I did, buddy. No way I wouldn't." I could wait till tomorrow to explain to him about Dad and Shelley. About going back to San Diego but coming sometimes to visit me. About being Andy again.

Holding his hand, I stood back up and looked around. Everyone was there—my teachers, my clients, my friends. Carol and Rafe. Even Ben!

"But you're in Alaska," I protested.

"Well, no. I'm here. North Star is in Alaska. And I'm flying back tomorrow. But I couldn't miss this."

Rafe stood there grinning. I shook a finger at him in a mock scolding. "You! What next? Are you going to set up as a psychic? You and your *what-ifs*?"

"Actually," said Ben, "I think I've persuaded him to go to law school."

Rafe looked a bit embarrassed. And pleased.

"But you said you wouldn't want to do what Ben does!" I blurted out. I realized too late how tactless that was. But Ben laughed.

"Very few lawyers litigate family law cases," he said. "Rafe can do any number of things—contracts, environmental law, research—"

"I'd like to stick to things that help people," Rafe said.

"Good," I said. "You can start by helping me file papers for my name change."

He looked startled. "What's your name going to be now?" he asked.

"Linda . . . Elaine . . . Farley. But," I added, "my friends can call me Lainie."

ANNE L. WATSON, a retired historic preservation architecture consultant, is the author of numerous novels, plus books on such diverse subjects as soapmaking and baking with cookie molds. She currently lives in Friday Harbor, Washington, in the San Juan Islands, with her husband and fellow author, Aaron Shepard. Please visit her at **www.annelwatson.com**.